THE CELEBRATED PEDESTRIAN

Suzanne Allain

LeMoyne House

Prologue

❧❧

The gentleman who came out of the inn and approached the start of his last mile, his thousandth, was a shell of his former self. His clothes hung upon his frame, his knee was wrapped in a bandage, and this man of thirty-seven, heretofore in his prime, walked as feebly as an eighty-year-old. This was his forty-second day without a decent night's sleep, forty-two days with no time to eat a normal meal. However, now that he approached the end of this test of endurance he found the strength to walk a little faster, and smiled and nodded at the crowds that had gathered to watch, most of whom had money riding on the outcome.

The *London Chronicle* had reported that it was impossible to perform such an act without overheating the blood and expiring on the spot. For weeks, eager spectators had gathered expecting to witness the death of Captain Richard Standham Wentworth, betting on his chances of success or failure, some even trying to sabotage him. His daughters, aged ten and seven, were not allowed to visit the course until today, the moment of their father's triumphant finish.

Faith scarcely recognized the man who was pointed out to her as her father and, though it had been explained to her that his goal was to walk one mile an hour for 1000 miles in succession, she could not understand the point of such an exercise. She found the crowds too noisy, the weather too hot, and the sight of her father walking slowly and painfully toward a post that marked the half mile point, excruciatingly boring.

She took out a book and began to read.

One

❧❧

London, England, June 1819

"Lord McElroy is such a graceful dancer," Mrs. Tibbet told her charge, nodding in the direction of her current quarry who was standing across the ballroom from them. Faith obediently looked in that direction, and then quickly looked away when it was obvious the man in question had noticed their gaze. Which was probably Mrs. Tibbet's intention in the first place. She was crafty, that Mrs. Tibbet. And desperate. Faith was not having a successful season and Mrs. Tibbet probably despaired of ever getting her off her hands. Still, to call Lord McElroy a beautiful dancer was preposterous.

"He has a club foot and only dances the Commencement," Faith replied.

"That proves my point exactly. To exude such modest elegance in spite of a disadvantage—well, I can't really call it a disadvantage, because it is part of what makes him who he is, the consummate gentleman."

"Next you'll be telling me his excesses at the gaming table are proof of his desire to give to the poor!"

"An excellent point. He's as generous a gentleman as ever was."

Faith stared at her chaperon in disbelief. Surely that last was said in an ironical manner? But no, Mrs.

Tibbet's protuberant, pale blue eyes, which were starting to feature prominently in Faith's nightmares, were gazing steadfastly into her own. Faith was the first to look away, although she was careful not to look in Lord McElroy's direction. She did not care if he did have £15,000 a year and estates in Ireland and England, something her chaperon had whispered into her ear on the last occasion they'd seen the gentleman. In Faith's opinion, Mrs. Tibbet should have been working at a bank in the city rather than escorting young women in society. She had an amazing memory for figures, but very little talent at making herself agreeable to others.

Faith was disappointed she could not like her chaperon, for she had looked forward to this season with great anticipation. Her father was a widower and both he and his late wife's family were country gentility with no connection to London society—at least, not any *feminine* society—so her father's idea to hire a chaperon had seemed like a good one. She had hoped her chaperon would be someone more attune to her own personality, but Mrs. Tibbet was consumed with her chore to a fault. Faith believed her chances would have been better had her chaperon *not* pushed her in the direction of every breathing, eligible male. Faith had no romantic experience with gentlemen, but she was raised in a male household and it seemed to her any man would run if pursued. Nevertheless, Mrs. Tibbet might as well have been a hound on the hunt.

As if Mrs. Tibbet sensed the direction of Faith's thoughts she suddenly sat up straighter in her chair, her nose pointed and twitching as if she'd just caught her prey's scent.

"Faith, I see a young gentleman I would like to introduce to you. Are your curls neat?" She turned to Faith and began plucking at her hair, while Faith helplessly submitted to the disarrangement of her coiffure.

"I think I've met enough young gentlemen tonight, Mrs. Tibbet. Indeed, I am ready to depart."

Her protests in vain, Faith was pulled from her seat and whisked across the ballroom. She kept her eyes cast downward, as she was embarrassed, and so unknowingly hid her best feature. She heard the man greet Mrs. Tibbet and ventured a peek at him. He was the most prepossessing of the gentlemen she'd met thus far, tall and fair-haired with tanned skin, but he had the same expression of polite resignation on his face that most of the gentlemen she'd been introduced to wore when tracked down by her chaperon. She fervently hoped it was her chaperon and not she herself who caused them to look that way.

"Sir Anthony Burke, may I introduce you to Miss Wentworth?"

"Miss Wentworth, a pleasure. You're not any connection to Captain Richard Standham Wentworth, by any chance?" His expression had changed, and now he seemed happy, even eager, to meet her.

Mrs. Tibbet shot her a warning glance. She had told Faith to deny the connection if asked, as she felt her father's notoriety would be a hindrance to Faith's acceptance by polite society. Faith had felt it best to comply with her chaperon's wishes in this regard, not because she agreed with her, but because she had lived in the shadow of her famous father her entire life and had wanted to be liked for her own merits. She had decided if the question arose she would just give a vague reply, saying something about "Wentworth" being a not uncommon surname. However, she knew if she replied that way now, Sir Anthony would politely excuse himself from her company and that would be the extent of their acquaintance. And she suddenly was possessed by the desire to have this gentleman's attention.

"He is my father," she told him, and was instantly rewarded.

"Miss Wentworth, may I have the pleasure of this dance?"

❧❧

Faith soon regretted her moment's impulse. Not at first, of course, when Sir Anthony led her to the floor and smiled charmingly at her. At that point she was congratulating herself on having captured such a handsome gentleman's interest. But very shortly after the dance began he turned the conversation to the subject of her father's sporting career, something she had discussed too often to find anything but a bore. Worse, still, she was beginning to think Sir Anthony thought of her only as a means to an end.

"I say," he said, as the dance steps brought them together and his hand lightly clasped her own, "perhaps you and your father would care to visit Kenilworth, my estate in Sussex. I have a nice set-up of my own he might like to see; quoits and dumbbells and the like. I could change it, of course, if it doesn't meet his requirements. I know he's the expert on such things, after all." And: "Did I tell you I lost quite a bit betting against him in '09? First and last time I underestimated him, I can tell you."

Faith could only nod; he spoke too quickly and eagerly for her to change the subject, and it would have been ill-mannered of her to interrupt. She could feel her face assuming the same look of polite resignation Sir Anthony's had when first approached by Mrs. Tibbet. She actually began to wish for the end of the set, and she dearly loved to dance.

"Miss Wentworth, may I please call on you tomorrow?"

"If you'd like. I cannot guarantee we will be at home, however. That is, I think I may have another appointment," she said, struggling over the polite fiction. She was horrid at making excuses. She saw that he looked surprised and she immediately relented. "That is, tomorrow is Thursday, is it not? I actually think it's on Friday that I have an appointment. If you're sure you have the time we will be at home tomorrow."

"I look forward to seeing you," he said, but she could see some of his excitement had faded. As had her own.

❧

Sir Anthony returned Miss Wentworth to her chaperon and joined a friend of his in the corner of the ballroom.

"You're not usually one to pay court to the latest new debutante," Sir Anthony's friend, Lord Frederick Brand, said to him after they'd exchanged greetings.

"You'll never guess who she is," Sir Anthony said

excitedly.

"You're correct. Who is she?"

"She's the daughter of Richard Standham Wentworth!"

Lord Frederick looked blank at first, as Wentworth's famous exploit had taken place ten years ago when Frederick was just fifteen, but as Wentworth had been the most talked-of celebrity of the last decade and had spurred a rash of imitators, he was soon able to recall him. "The gentleman who walked 1000 miles in 1000 hours? She doesn't appear to resemble him very much. I would have expected a daughter of his to be a strapping, burly girl. She looks very feminine. Delicate, even. What did you think of her?"

"What?" Sir Anthony was having a difficult time remembering what the lady looked like, and quickly gave up the effort. "Oh, nice enough, I suppose. I was just so impressed that I was dancing with the daughter of The Celebrated Pedestrian himself!"

"She did dance rather well. Must have inherited some of her father's famous footwork."

"Did she? Can't say I noticed. We were talking mostly of the Captain. I invited them to my estate."

"Really?" Lord Frederick asked. "That taken with her, were you? She seemed pretty enough from where I was standing, but I've never seen you bowled over by a female so quickly before."

"Oh, well, I wasn't that impressed with her at first; she was with that harridan Mrs. Tibbet and my first thought was to run for my life. That woman won't be happy until she's married off everyone of her acquaintance. I don't know why, exactly. I don't recall her and Mr. Tibbet being an example of marital bliss." He shuddered. "Actually, I can't imagine how Mr. Tibbet could stand those eyes over breakfast every morning. She reminds me of a fish."

"What color are Miss Wentworth's eyes?"

"How should I know? I told her about my set-up at Kenilworth. She seemed impressed. Now that I think on it, I should have asked her about her father's regimen. My friend Clough, you remember him? He walked 300 miles in less than five days once for a wager but turned up lame. Won his bet, though. He highly recommends purging but I'm not sure I trust his recipe. I wonder if Miss Wentworth knows the Captain's recipe."

"You'd never discuss purging with that lovely girl!"

"I suppose you're right. Might not be quite the thing. Better wait until I meet her father." Sir Anthony was silent a moment, awed by his good fortune. "Never would have thought, never would even have *dreamt*, that I'd have the opportunity of meeting The Celebrated Pedestrian. And to think he'll be a guest in my home!"

"If you do manage to convince them to come, can I wangle an invitation as well?"

"Of course, of course. I know you're just as excited as I about meeting him."

"Quite right," Lord Frederick said, managing to contain his exclamations of delight at the prospect.

Two
❧❧

Faith thought she'd been punished enough for her hasty decision to reveal her identity to Sir Anthony the previous evening; however, the next day she found that her suffering had only just begun.

When Sir Anthony came for his morning call, Mrs. Tibbit succeeded in persuading him (although not a lot of persuasion was necessary) to take Faith for a ride in his curricle. Faith was submitted to a half-hour litany of its features in meticulous detail. She comprehended very little of this exhaustive discourse, not being in the market for a curricle nor currently employed as a carriage maker, and found it almost as boring as Sir Anthony's second topic of conversation: every wager he had won by beating someone else's time from Here to There and back again. He assumed, as her father was a renowned sportsman and a noted whip, that she would find this conversation as fascinating as he did himself.

Faith was unsure if Sir Anthony even recognized she was someone of the feminine persuasion. It appeared he thought of her as merely a surrogate for her father until that gentleman could somehow be produced. His conversation was laced with comments such as: "Your father might be interested to know," or "You might just mention to your father.," etc. etc. She wondered if Sir Anthony expected her to be taking notes! Faith was tempted to say: "Indeed, my father might be interested but I am most certainly not." She was very close to succumbing to temptation when there was an interruption in the form of a lone gentleman rider approaching the carriage.

Faith directed a blinding smile in his direction, so happy that her specific form of purgatory was coming to an end, and then she wondered if the gentleman misread her smile as a form of encouragement because he gave her *such* a look. She shut her fan with a snap and began fiddling with her gloves. Sir Anthony introduced his friend as Lord Frederick Brand and, the formalities observed, Lord Frederick began to walk his horse alongside his friend's curricle.

"Have you been in town long, Miss Wentworth?"

"Since the start of the season, Lord Frederick."

"I'm surprised we have not met prior to this. The season is almost at its end."

"Yes, it goes by rather quickly, does it not? So many entertainments."

"Said with the jaded sophistication of someone who has spent many seasons in town. But this is your first London season, am I correct?"

"Do I wear my history on my sleeve?" Faith asked, extending her arm and glancing down at it.

"No, I must admit Sir Anthony has been relating some of your circumstances to me."

"Yes, Miss Wentworth, Lord Frederick also greatly admires your father," Sir Anthony said, wondering how he'd lost the reins of such a promising conversation and trying to steer it back in the proper direction.

"Indeed. And yet I do not think you have met him, have you Lord Frederick?" The smile Faith had been wearing vanished, and there was a challenge in her expression and tone of voice. There was a slight pause as Lord Frederick met her look for look.

"I am not acquainted with your father, Miss Wentworth. However, any man who lays claim to such a beautiful daughter must be worthy of admiration."

Faith dropped her gaze and tried to will herself not to blush. She felt she'd forced him into such a compliment with her silly sensitivity about her father. "I'm not sure I'd agree with you, Lord Frederick. Surely beauty is but an accident of nature and not the result of any admirable trait on the part of one's parents?" Realizing that could be construed as a vain acceptance of his compliment, she rushed back into speech. "I meant to speak in generalities merely, as I'm persuaded you are intent on flattering me."

"I am greatly offended. Do I appear to you after such a short acquaintance as a heartless rogue bent upon flattering all the ladies?"

Faith surveyed him gravely, one finger to her chin as if in deep contemplation. "I must confess, this being only my first season, that I am still unfamiliar with the ways of heartless rogues. And it has always been my maxim to 'judge not by appearances.'"

Sir Anthony, tired of being ignored, jumped back into the conversation, to the surprise of his companions, who had been thoroughly engrossed in their conversation to the exclusion of their surroundings. "Oh, Lord Frederick is not a rogue at all. Actually more of a sportsman, like myself. Not to be compared with your father, of course."

"Of course," Faith murmured, a little deflated. She was enjoying Lord Frederick's company and hated to think that his attentions to her might be for the same reason as Sir Anthony's, although more cleverly disguised. Maybe he was a heartless rogue, after all. He certainly had the appearance of one.

For, though Sir Anthony was quite handsome, Lord Frederick was undeniably attractive as well, and in a way somehow more appealing to Faith than Sir Anthony's fair good looks. Lord Frederick had dark hair and eyes and was also tall and well-built, though not quite as broad-shouldered as Sir Anthony. Perhaps she was just susceptible to flirtatious glances and extravagant compliments and should be on her guard. Mrs. Tibbet's advice to her about how to interact with gentlemen had been such a confusing mix of propriety and predaciousness that Faith was left feeling unsure of herself, as she was uncertain about her own judgment in such matters. She sat back in her seat as Sir Anthony engaged Lord Frederick in a conversation about his horse.

❧

Faith would have been very surprised to learn where Lord Frederick's true interest lay, and that he was wishing Sir Anthony to the Devil almost as fervently as she was. He was actually paying very little attention to Sir Anthony's conversation whilst covertly studying Miss Wentworth.

He had first noticed her at a musicale they had both attended about a sennight ago. She had been sitting directly across the room from him and he, bored by a particularly long performance on the harp, had observed that while the rest of the company fidgeted and yawned she sat with quiet dignity, even as her chaperone whispered and twitched beside her.

He had thought her very attractive from afar, noting that she had fine eyes and a handsome figure, and had hoped for an opportunity to observe her more closely. However, he was aware of her chaperone's reputation and was daunted by the fact that Mrs. Tibbet would undoubtedly leap on any interest he might show. So he had continued to watch Faith over the next week, never approaching her, but becoming more and more impressed with her poise and decorum, which seemed in stark contrast to her companion's lack thereof.

When Sir Anthony had danced with her at last night's ball, Lord Frederick was surprised by the pang of jealousy he had felt. He had seen Miss Wentworth's smile at Sir Anthony's attention, and had deduced that she had initially been attracted to the handsome baronet. However, as the dance progressed, he saw her face assume a similar expression to that which she wore when accompanied by her ill-mannered chaperone. It had made him curious about what Sir Anthony had done to provoke such a reaction. Even now he sensed a similar reserve, and realized that she must not share her father's interest in sports. This was not surprising to him, as it was not considered part of a lady's domain, but apparently Sir Anthony was not as discerning as he.

Mostly to spare the lady any further boredom, Lord Frederick cut Sir Anthony's conversation short and made his departure. But he found that his interest in

Miss Wentworth had not diminished upon closer observation. If anything, he found himself even further impressed with the young lady. She stirred a chivalrous instinct in him as he sensed a loneliness about her, and he wondered if it was caused by the world's interest in her famous parent. Lord Frederick had seen her displeasure when Sir Anthony introduced Captain Wentworth into the conversation, and thought how difficult it must be to always be thought of as someone's daughter, rather than a person in your own right.

As for Lord Frederick, he found the daughter far more intriguing.

❧

When she returned to the house with Sir Anthony after their drive, Faith found herself in a very dangerous position. Sir Anthony's infatuation with her father had reached such a pitch that he was throwing all caution to the winds. He made the mistake of issuing Faith an invitation to his house party once again, and this time in the hearing of Mrs. Tibbet and her callers. It was like waving a choice bone in front of a hungry dog.

Mrs. Tibbet directed a look dripping with significance at one matron, Mrs. Howard, whose daughter was gazing longingly in Sir Anthony's direction. "Sir Anthony is *so* eager to meet Miss Wentworth's father," Mrs. Tibbet told her callers.

"It is one of my fondest hopes," Sir Anthony agreed eagerly, unconcerned with how his words could be misconstrued by matchmaking mothers. In his mind, all the world shared his obsession with the illustrious Captain Wentworth.

Faith shot him a look of warning, but he had risen and begun taking his leave and failed to see it. Once he was gone, Miss Howard congratulated Faith on her conquest through gritted teeth.

Faith no longer wanted any attention at all from Sir Anthony, having quickly discerned where his true interest lay. She realized she could not continue spending time with him without society anticipating an engagement, but apparently Sir Anthony was too foolish to reach a similar conclusion. He continued to dance attendance on her at all the entertainments they attended, even asking Mrs. Tibbet which invitations they planned to accept, and he took Faith riding in his curricle twice more, even when she tried to fob him off with excuses.

One week after their initial meeting, as Sir Anthony approached Faith and Mrs. Tibbet upon their arrival at a ball, Faith experienced the heretofore unknown pleasure of having her chaperone's unalloyed approval. Beaming upon them both, Mrs. Tibbet acquiesced playfully to Sir Anthony's request for Miss Wentworth's hand for the next dance.

"I would never stand in the way of two young people like yourselves dancing together, or pursuing any other endeavor in which you might be well-matched," she said, and guffawed at her very poor attempt at a joke.

Sir Anthony thanked her and led Faith out for the dance, but he was frowning when Lord Frederick approached him soon afterward.

"You don't look very happy for a man on the verge of an engagement," Lord Frederick said. He tried to say it jokingly, but there was an edge to his tone. He wished he'd not allowed Mrs. Tibbet's reputation to deter him from pursuing Miss Wentworth when he'd first noticed her. Now it appeared as if he'd have to see her wed to his friend.

"What! Have you lost your mind?" Sir Anthony looked around fearfully, to verify there was no one within hearing distance.

"Not to worry. *I* am not the one spreading rumors of your approaching nuptials."

"What rumors? It's Tibbet the Terrible, isn't it? I'd never seen her teeth before this evening. It took me a while to work out she was smiling; I thought she was about to bite. But it's obvious she's got some bee in her bonnet—"

"It's not groundless, after all. You've been pursuing Miss Wentworth single-mindedly the past week. Tibbet's not the one who began the rumors, although I'm sure she's wasted no time in fanning the flames."

Sir Anthony turned a trifle pale and looked as if he might be sick. "You're right! What was I thinking? I totally forgot Miss Wentworth is a young lady."

"That does seem inconceivable to me. I don't think I could spend so much time in Miss Wentworth's company and forget she was a lady. At least, not in the manner you did."

Sir Anthony groaned audibly. It was Lord Frederick's turn to look around, and then direct him toward a nearby doorway that led to a terrace. The cool night air seemed to revive Sir Anthony a little, although he still appeared to be in a state of considerable mental distress. He had dropped his head into his hands, but after a few minutes he looked up and assumed a resolute stance. "I suppose I will have to marry her. There's no honorable way out of it." He looked hopefully at his friend. "Unless you can think of something?"

"Buck up; maybe she'll refuse you."

"Not she; any protégé of Mrs. Tibbet will jump at the chance to put a noose around my neck."

"I must insist you do not speak of the young lady in such an insulting manner in my presence. You've egregiously misjudged her twice in less than a sennight: first, as nothing more then a cipher in a skirt; and now as a harpy like her chaperone. Please admit that you know nothing of her true character."

Sir Anthony was not a very astute young gentleman, but even he recognized from his friend's fierce expression and the tone of his voice he had angered him. He opened and closed his mouth twice but could not form an intelligible sentence. Finally he said, "I beg your pardon."

Lord Frederick simply nodded his forgiveness. There was a long silence while Sir Anthony eyed him suspiciously. Finally, in the tone of a man making a scientific discovery, he said: "You fancy her yourself!"

"And why shouldn't I? Not every gentleman is as purblind as you. I find her very…attractive."

Sir Anthony began to smile. "Thank the Lord for that. I'll gladly step aside. I'll even stand up for you at the wedding—"

"I did not say I wanted to marry her; I've only just met her. But I *would* like to spend more time in her company before she's marched off to the altar willy-nilly with you."

"Then we're both destined for disappointment. Tibbet is ready to collect payment for services rendered. She's not going to let this opportunity slip through her fingers."

Sir Anthony fell into a morose silence while Lord Frederick pondered the matter. "Maybe this house party of yours isn't such a bad idea," he finally said, breaking the silence. "If you rounded out the invitation list; invited some other eligible young ladies and gentlemen."

"But then I'll have to give a ball and arrange dinner parties and nonsense like that! I had such plans for Captain Wentworth and myself. Did you know he once lifted a man who weighed over 16 stone with one hand? There's a technique to his pedestrianism, as well: I hear he walks bent slightly forward so as to spare his ankles extra wear."

"I'm sorry you and Captain Wentworth will not be walking off into the sunset together, but you have other issues to deal with at the moment. Now, I assume *I* am invited? Do you have a hostess?"

"My mother will do it, I suppose. Although if she catches the scent of orange blossom she'll be hand-in-glove with The Tibbet. She's anxious to see me leg-shackled, as well."

"Does Miss Wentworth have any sisters? Maybe one of them will lift *you* with one hand and you'll fall head-over-heels. Literally."

Three

❧❧

Faith did indeed have a sister, although at times she wished she did not. Her younger sister, while close to her in age, was her extreme opposite in disposition. Whereas Faith confined her interests quite happily to those that were considered within a young lady's domain, and genuinely enjoyed those activities, her sister Charity was intent on following her father's and brothers' gentlemanly pursuits with a vigor that was not considered appropriate for a young lady, particularly by that young lady's father.

He had done his duty by his daughters when, upon the death of his wife on the occasion of Charity's birth, he had handed them over to a series of nannies and governesses who had come highly recommended and could be expected to raise two girls without inconveniencing him in the least. But Charity defied him from the start, as she frequently escaped from her guardians' charge and turned up in the stables, or a tree, or didn't turn up at all, causing all in the household to abandon their activities and make a frantic search for her. As a young child she often screamed for hours, the sound reverberating through Captain Wentworth's otherwise peaceful abode, and she never could keep her clothing unsoiled or even intact.

The girls' governess frequently told them that as two females with no mother in a household of males they were to look to each other for comfort, but Faith found Charity was far more likely to pull her curls than brush them for her. When a very devout nanny assigned them to commit part of the Bible to memory, Faith used to quote chapter 13 of Paul's epistle to the Corinthians very zealously to her sister:

"Charity suffereth long, and is kind; charity envieth not; doth not behave itself unseemly, is not easily provoked, thinketh no evil."

Faith was never sure if it was for this reason or some other that Charity despised her given name and by sheer force of will had induced her family and intimate acquaintance to call her "Cherry" instead. Faith had no problem calling her sister by her chosen diminutive, as she felt it suited her far better than her given name.

Hence it was with no feeling of surprise, but rather with a familiar sense of resignation, that Faith read a letter she'd received from her father the next morning at breakfast, telling her of his displeasure with her sister's behavior and requesting that Faith return home.

"I realize that you had planned to spend another fortnight in town," the letter read, in part, "however, I believe your sister's character too weak and still in need of the beneficial example you set in behavior suited to a young lady. If you were to return and attempt again to coax her into more genteel pursuits, I believe she might prove more conformable than on past occasions. I found it necessary to sternly reprove and reproach her for her latest conduct, and I do find her manner more subdued than usual."

Faith didn't wonder that Cherry's behavior was subdued; she idolized her famous father and to hear him reproach her must have greatly sunk her spirits. However, Faith did not believe, as her father apparently did, that such reproof would have any kind of lasting effect. Nor did she feel that her own example exerted any type of influence on her sister, and particularly not a "beneficial" one. She put the letter down and turned to Mrs. Tibbet, who had been watching her with ill-concealed curiosity.

"What is the news from home?" Mrs. Tibbet asked.

"My father would like me to return home and assist him with my sister, and I think that I should acquiesce to his wishes."

"What? Return home? That would be folly indeed! Captain Wentworth has no idea how that would harm your chances with Sir Anthony. I had intended to write him this very morning and ask his permission to escort you to Sir Anthony's estate."

"Mrs. Tibbet, I appreciate your efforts in my behalf, but this may be the best solution for all concerned. Even if Sir Anthony were to offer me marriage, which is highly doubtful, I have no intention of accepting. So to return home would quiet any gossip that might have arisen from his attentions, such as they were," Faith said, with a slight curl of her lip. She never really felt she'd had any "attention" from Sir Anthony at all.

"You cannot be serious in what you say! I am on the verge of catching for you a most advantageous match. You do not have to bestir yourself in the least; just accept this invitation to his house party and your future is secured. I cannot imagine, should I write your father and inform him of how circumstances stand, that he'd still desire you to return home. In fact, I'm sure he would not desire it in the least!"

"He might not, but that doesn't change the fact that I do!" Faith said, irritated that what Mrs. Tibbet said was true. If she did receive an offer from Sir Anthony, it would not have been because of any virtue or attractions she herself possessed, but rather her surname and the talk promoted by Mrs. Tibbet. She had not formerly rated her attractions so low, but after a season in town with Mrs. Tibbet she was beginning to doubt her own worth. Her father's letter had seemed providential in its timing; she was suddenly possessed of no stronger desire than to return home and remove herself from so humiliating a situation, and such depressing company.

Faith was aware that her appearance in London accompanied by Mrs. Tibbet had spoiled her chances from the start; Mrs. Tibbet's character was too different from Faith's, and no gentleman drawn to Faith's more subtle personality would be able to overlook her chaperon's brash presence. If Faith was more confident she might have been able to assert her own personality more, but her mother had died when she was three years old and she felt her knowledge of polite society might somehow be lacking as a result. Mrs. Tibbet was older and, theoretically, wiser, and Faith felt she shouldn't disregard Mrs. Tibbet's instruction, but neither was she comfortable following it. She was determined to bring an end to this ordeal and, if she ever attempted another season, would insist on approving her chaperon herself and not relying on her father to engage someone.

Faith was sure there was no part of her London season she'd regret leaving behind, when Lord Frederick's face flashed into her mind's eye for a moment. She wished she had met him under different circumstances, or that she'd somehow have the opportunity to meet him again in the future, but she quickly dismissed such hopes as absurd. He was obviously not interested in pursuing the acquaintance. It was true that he had called once while she was out riding with Sir Anthony, but one call was not indicative of serious interest, and he had not called again. She had no way of knowing that Mrs. Tibbet had dropped a very unsubtle hint to Lord Frederick that Faith would soon be engaged to Sir Anthony, and he had given up his pursuit as hopeless.

"You are too young to realize what is in your best interests," Mrs. Tibbet said, dismissing Faith's wish to return home with a wave of her hand. "I will write to your father. Perhaps Miss Charity can join us at the house party under my auspices."

Faith could read Mrs. Tibbet's mind with startling accuracy: She was figuring in her head the price she could charge for marrying off *two* of Captain Wentworth's daughters at one blow.

❧❧

Faith soon found she had no choice in the matter; her strength of will was no match for Mrs. Tibbet's, and Mrs. Tibbet appeared deaf to anything Faith had to say on the subject. Faith was now committed to attending the house party, and Mrs. Tibbet had even arranged for Captain Wentworth to meet them there with Cherry in tow. But Faith was encouraged to learn that she and her family were not the only guests who were to be in attendance. Perhaps it would no longer appear that Sir Anthony was singling her out for special attention.

She discovered this while attending the opera with Mrs. Tibbet and her nephew, a young man who was connected on his father's side to an Earl and so featured largely in Mrs. Tibbet's conversation. This was Faith's first encounter with him and she found herself unimpressed. He was a pallid, quiet boy of nineteen who would not meet her eyes and barely spoke, even when asked a direct question. Faith could only surmise that being related to Mrs. Tibbet had made him wary of any female. So it was with a great deal of relief that she greeted Sir Anthony and Lord Frederick when they appeared at her box during the intermission.

She found Sir Anthony changed in some way, and she eventually realized it was because he was addressing most of his conversation to Mrs. Tibbet and her nephew, and not subjecting Faith to a monologue about her father or his favorite sport. Faith turned eagerly toward Lord Frederick, thankful to escape her erstwhile companions.

Lord Frederick was bowled over by the smile Faith directed at him, and it took him a moment to respond to her greeting.

"Good evening, Miss Wentworth. You are looking quite handsome this evening." He felt it was an understatement of major proportions. Some of her dark hair had escaped from its upward swirl and contrasted delightfully with the long, white column of her neck. He had finally ascertained her eyes were grey, but when she wore green, as she did this evening, they reflected that color.

"Thank you, Lord Frederick. But you could say that of everyone tonight," she said, gesturing at the theatre boxes that surrounded them. And it was quite a stunning vista, with women in silks and satins glistening in the gas-light.

"It is a lovely sight, it's true. But not everyone appears to such advantage upon closer inspection," he murmured, turning back to look at Faith. She found she could not meet his gaze, so intense was his stare. She felt somehow that it was improper for him to look at her so, but she had no idea how to stop him and was unsure if she wanted to.

There was an awkward silence, which finally succeeded in bringing Lord Frederick to his senses. "I hear that you are to be a guest at Sir Anthony's estate in Sussex," he said.

If Miss Wentworth was excited at the prospect, she hid it well, merely nodding in reply. If anything, the thought appeared to depress her.

"I only mention it," Lord Frederick continued, "because I, too, will be attending the house party."

Her head whipped around at his comment and she smiled. "I am so pleased to hear it. Is it to be a large party?"

"Sir Anthony's mother, of course, will be hostess, and I do believe the Perrywhistle family will be there. I am not sure if you are acquainted with them?"

"We have not been introduced, though I have seen them around town." Faith was so happy to hear there were other guests she would not have cared if they were gypsies, but she had always thought Miss Perry-whistle looked like a decent sort of girl, and wished she might know her better.

"Sir Anthony tells me that your father will also attend."

"Yes, along with my younger sister, Miss Charity Wentworth."

"Is your younger sister as virtuous as her name implies?"

"It would be *uncharitable* of me to comment," Faith said, and Lord Frederick smiled in response to her pun. "You shall have to wait and meet my sister and decide for yourself."

"I look forward to it."

Four

❧❧

"We have arrived, Faith. I am hopeful that the next time I visit Sir Anthony's estate you will be greeting me as its hostess."

Faith turned from the carriage window where she had been peering with mingled curiosity and trepidation at Sir Anthony's home to speak earnestly to her chaperone. "Mrs. Tibbet, I appreciate your efforts in my behalf but I must tell you yet again that I am not interested in marrying Sir Anthony and view this visit as merely a pleasant interlude in the country."

"You are a stubborn, willful, and ungrateful girl, and you do not deserve this good fortune. However, I am here to look after your best interests, like it or not. So we will speak no more of this for now. Mind your step."

A footman opened the carriage door and Faith stepped down. Sir Anthony's house, Kenilworth, loomed before her. She noted it was attractive and the grounds well-kept, yet she couldn't help but feel it menacing. She could envision the columns that graced the front of the house as prison bars, threatening to incarcerate her in a half-life similar to the one she'd always lived; her days spent in polite acceptance of people and things that held no interest for her, while longing to escape into a world where she did belong.

But after being ushered into an elegant drawing

room by the butler and announced to her hostess, Lady
Burke, she found herself dismissing her fears as foolish.
This woman, with her kind smile and her understanding
eyes, would never permit any harm to come to Faith in
her household. Faith felt herself beginning to relax under her maternal gaze, and wondered if the house party
she so dreaded might actually prove to be enjoyable.

"Miss Wentworth, how happy I am to have you
as a guest in my home. I so hope you enjoy a comfortable stay with us." Lady Burke directed Faith to sit near
her on the sofa, and Faith happily complied with her
wishes.

"I am sure I will be very comfortable, thank you,
Lady Burke."

"It will be so wonderful to have some feminine
company again. I have two daughters who have married
and left me; one last season and one the season before. I
know that it is supposed to be every mother's ambition
to see her daughters married, but I am sure I do not
know why. I must be very selfish, indeed, but I'd have
preferred to enjoy my daughters' company for as long as
possible."

Mrs. Tibbet tittered. "Lady Burke you are so
droll. Of course we know you cannot really mean it. I
hear your elder daughter is now the Marchioness of
Trent. *Such* a good match. Welbourn Abbey has to be
the most prosperous estate in Derbyshire."

"But it is, as you say, in *Derbyshire*. That does
not at all reconcile me to the match. There must be
dozens of estimable young gentlemen here in Sussex. I
venture to say that a few live within a ten mile drive.
Why she couldn't have had the good sense to fall in love

with one of them, I'm sure I cannot say."

"It was quite perverse of her, I agree," Faith said, smiling at her hostess. "But perhaps you can divide your time between Derbyshire and Sussex."

"But you forget I have another daughter, and she now lives in Cornwall. It is too bad of them. It looks as if I'm to spend most of my declining years shuttling about in a carriage."

Lady Burke spoke rather playfully, so Faith was aware that she was not entirely serious when she complained of her daughters' marriages. Mrs. Tibbet, however, could never imagine that Lady Burke would not take such matters as seriously as a funeral service, and as it was common knowledge in town that the younger had not made as sterling a match as the elder, she prepared to commiserate with the unfortunate Lady Burke.

"It is too bad about your younger daughter. I am surprised you did not forbid the match. I hear Cornwall is a sadly primitive place, with no society, and that her husband is a man of limited means."

"Other than the distance that separates us, I have nothing to complain of in her choice. My daughter's husband is a man of integrity."

"And I hear Cornwall has a very beautiful coast. I quite long to visit," Faith hurried to interject, as it was obvious Lady Burke was displeased by Mrs. Tibbet's remark.

Lady Burke's frown disappeared, and she smiled at Faith. "Do you enjoy travel then, my dear?"

"I have not had the opportunity thus far in my life, but it has always interested me greatly. I must confess that the only travel I do now is through the pages of a book."

"You must help yourself to our library while you are here. My husband amassed a large collection before his death, and you are sure to find many travel books among them."

"Thank you, Lady Burke. It is most kind of you. Reading is one of my favorite pastimes, but I do not have the opportunity to indulge in it as much as I'd like. My father's tastes run contrary to my own, so our library is composed almost entirely of stud books, books about pugilism, and copies of the *Sporting Magazine*."

"I understand. Sir Anthony has a similar fascination with the Fancy. I find it a trifle tedious, I must admit."

Lady Burke's smile was warmly sympathetic and Faith wanted to clap her hands in glee. She had never before met anyone who had no desire to discuss her father's career with her. Everyone she met assumed it must be her favorite topic of conversation. Even her sister, who might be expected to find the subject as boring as Faith did, spoke of almost nothing else.

Mrs. Tibbet, while not at all interested in sports, had a similar tendency to focus on one topic to the exclusion of all else. When she heard Sir Anthony's name mentioned, she realized this was her opportunity to redirect the conversation to her own interests.

"Miss Wentworth and I could never find Sir Anthony tedious. Your son is a true gentleman, so aware of all those attentions that we ladies find so necessary to our well-being. Why, there was barely a day that passed this last sennight that we did not find him in our parlor. His concern for my charge became quite the talk of the town."

It was obvious Faith was made uncomfortable by her chaperon's words, and her happy expression faded. Lady Burke watched Faith in silence for a moment, before replying to Mrs. Tibbet.

"I am pleased to hear Sir Anthony behaved as he ought. He can act far too impetuously at times. However, he did very well inviting Miss Wentworth here to distract me from my daughters' absence. And I must thank you, too, Mrs. Tibbet, for escorting Miss Wentworth. It was kind of you to make the trip. I have had a room prepared for you tonight, so that you can rest before returning to town tomorrow."

"Returning to town," Mrs. Tibbet repeated, looking shocked. "I hadn't thought to return to town so soon—"

"You are welcome to stay longer, but I assumed you would want to use our carriage, rather than return by post. It is available tomorrow, but I cannot guarantee that it will be available at the end of the house party, when Sir Anthony will have need of it. Also, I had hoped you would perform a small commission for me. My daughter, the Marchioness of Trent, is in town, and I need to send her a small item she requested. If you could call on her after returning to town she, and I, would be so *very* grateful."

Faith held her breath, afraid to hope that Mrs. Tibbet might actually leave. She knew by her chaperone's unusual silence she was deliberating the advantages and disadvantages of such a choice. The cost to hire a post chaise was an important consideration, as well as the promised introduction to the Marchioness of Trent. It could never hurt to have such a one beholden to her.

"Of course, if you would like to stay for the house party," Lady Burke continued, "you are very welcome, as I said. We are a trifle cramped at the moment, and you will probably have to share your room with the youngest Miss Perrywhistle, but she is a very well-behaved young miss, and her governess will sleep with her, so there is no fear of her disturbing you in the night."

Mrs. Tibbet looked daunted at the thought of sharing her room with two others, and Faith began a refrain of *Please, please, please* in her head.

"You are kind to invite me to stay," Mrs. Tibbet finally replied, "but it is true I have much to do in town. I think I will return in the morning, once I have spoken to Captain Wentworth, that is. I believe he will be arriving later this afternoon?"

Faith could scarcely believe her hopes had been realized, and resolved to pay Mrs. Tibbet out of her own allowance if her father would not. She was wise enough to realize Mrs. Tibbet would not think of leaving until she had finalized her arrangement with Captain Wentworth and received payment.

"Yes, we expect them before dinner," Lady Burke said. "Dinner is at six o'clock, but we will have a cold collation in the drawing room around two. Perhaps you would like to retire to your rooms until that time and refresh yourselves? I have had the footmen take your trunks to your rooms, and Simmons is waiting in the hall to direct you there."

"That would be lovely, as I assume Miss Perrywhistle is not in residence as of yet?"

"No, the Perrywhistles arrive tomorrow," Lady Burke hurried to assure Mrs. Tibbet.

"Splendid. I will retire to my chamber."

Mrs. Tibbet rose to leave and Faith also stood, sending her hostess a look brimming with gratitude as she did so. "Thank you so much for your hospitality, Lady Burke."

"It is truly my pleasure. I look forward to furthering our acquaintance."

❧

Faith was pleased to find when she came down to the drawing room later that afternoon that she had preceded her chaperon. She realized Mrs. Tibbet must still be resting in her room, giving Faith an unexpected break from her presence. She smiled happily at her hostess, who invited Faith to sit down and poured her a glass of orgeat.

"Sir Anthony and Lord Frederick will be joining us momentarily. They arrived while you were still upstairs."

Faith had mixed feelings about her hostess's announcement. She did enjoy Lord Frederick's company, what little of it she'd had thus far, but Sir Anthony was bound to dominate the conversation as he always did, and Faith would miss out on this rare opportunity to have an enjoyable conversation with someone who shared *her* interests.

"It will be lovely to see them both again," Faith replied dutifully.

"Yes, though they will interrupt our little tête-à-tête," Lady Burke said, and Faith wondered how she'd read her mind so accurately. "However, we have many weeks to spend together, and the gentlemen will no doubt be leaving us quite frequently to our own devices, so I'm sure we will have many more opportunities to become better acquainted."

Faith only had time to nod her agreement before they were interrupted by the arrival of the gentlemen, with Mrs. Tibbet on their heels. They had just all sat down again when Faith's sister arrived.

She was announced by the butler and the gentlemen stood at her entrance. Faith wondered why Cherry entered the drawing room alone. Where was their father?

Faith introduced her sister to Lady Burke, who asked Cherry if she would care to join them or prefer to retire to her room.

"If you would like to rest, Cherry, I can escort you to your room," Faith interjected. Her little sister looked quite intimidated by the exalted company in which she found herself. "Is Papa not with you?"

"No, he left this morning before dawn, and sent me with Mrs. Smith. He is walking and intends to arrive later this evening."

"Walking?" Sir Anthony exclaimed. "You don't say! Isn't your home a good eighty miles away?"

"Eighty-two," Cherry said, smiling brightly at Sir Anthony, her shyness melting away in her eagerness to discuss her father's athletic ability. "And the terrain is not at all even. He's covered such a distance more than once in 16 hours, but I'd lay odds he will beat that time."

"What kind of odds will you give?" Sir Anthony asked.

"Anthony, hush. This is not the kind of welcome we give guests in our home. Miss Wentworth is not one of your gambling cronies." Faith was very relieved Lady Burke interrupted, because she could envision Cherry requesting a betting book and recording the wager then and there. "Miss Charity," Lady Burke continued, "some refreshments would probably do you good. Please join us."

Faith watched her sister as she accepted Lady Burke's invitation with a shy smile. It appeared that Lady Burke's kindness could soften even Cherry's thorny exterior. She knew her sister was unused to polite company, though she had received instruction on proper behavior from Faith and their governess, a long-suffering woman who'd endured much mischief from Cherry. However, Cherry was still only seventeen, and much more comfortable outdoors than in a drawing room. Faith was relieved that someone had seen to it that Cherry's hair and nails were clean, and she was wearing a suitable gown, but she strode over to the settee with long strides that made Faith wince, and she had obviously taken no great pains with her appearance.

Faith tried to view her sister objectively, as if seeing her for the first time as the rest of the guests were, and she realized that her sister was quite attractive. She had lighter hair than Faith, but it was still a rich, honey-colored brown, and she was taller than Faith, with a slender, athletic figure. Her skin was a little too brown, as she hated to wear a sunbonnet and she spent most of her time out-of-doors, but her complexion was good, even though darker than the current mode.

"Are you very fatigued from the journey, Miss Charity?" Lady Burke asked.

"Oh no, my lady, not at all. I would have much preferred to walk, like Papa, but he insisted I take the carriage."

"So you share your father's pedestrian abilities?" Sir Anthony asked Cherry.

"I cannot claim to be as great an athlete, and he rarely permits me to accompany him on long journeys, but I do walk at least ten miles every day, and if ladies were permitted to engage in pedestrian contests, I do believe I would prove a worthy competitor. Indeed, I think I'd make better time than most gentlemen, even hampered by these skirts." Cherry cast a look of disgust at her feminine attire, and Faith wanted to sink in shame. But it appeared that most of the company was inclined to indulge Faith's sister in her peculiarities. Lady Burke and Lord Frederick appeared more amused than shocked, and Sir Anthony found nothing at all alarming about Cherry's speech, and asked her what the walking was like around their estate.

Before she had time to answer, Mrs. Tibbet had entered the conversation, her distaste for Cherry's speech evident. "Miss Charity is still rather young, and overly indulged by her father. I'm sure you'll overlook any peculiarity of manner or speech in someone barely out of the schoolroom."

Faith was afraid such a statement would provoke an even more embarrassing reply from Cherry, but was surprised when her sister looked stricken, turned red, and put her head down, murmuring what appeared to be an apology. Faith had no idea that the Captain had given Cherry strict instruction only to mention "feminine fripperies in the drawing room, or the weather" and that if she failed, he would dispatch her to a ladies' seminary for a year, a fate Cherry considered almost worse than death.

Faith and Lord Frederick spoke at once, in an attempt to break the awkward silence.

"I, myself, enjoy a good walk," Lord Frederick said, while Faith asked, "Are we very far from the village here?"

"Pardon me, Miss Wentworth."

"Not at all, you were saying?" Faith asked, with a smile at Lord Frederick, pleased that he would attempt to rescue her little sister.

"I think we were thinking along similar lines. That is, if you propose to walk to the village while you are staying at Kenilworth?"

"Yes, I wondered if the village were within convenient walking distance?"

"It depends upon what you consider convenient," Lady Burke said. "I am not as vigorous a walker as you young ladies, so I prefer these days to take the gig, but it's less than two miles on foot. They have quite a nice milliner's, if you ladies care to shop while you are here, and the church is worth touring."

Faith knew her sister had about as much interest in a milliner's shop as having a tooth drawn, but she was pleased to see her sister resume her composure and nod in response to Lady Burke's suggestion.

Conversation proceeded a little more smoothly afterward, although Mrs. Tibbet managed to cast a pall on things at every conceivable opportunity. Faith would have been amused if she could have heard Sir Anthony's comments to his mother about Mrs. Tibbet after the afternoon party broke up and the guests retired to their rooms to dress for dinner.

"That woman is insufferable. She makes more speeches than a country parson, and every one designed to make its hearer more miserable than the last. Poor Cherry Wentworth! She didn't deserve the treatment she received."

Lady Burke looked surprised at her son's remark. "I would think the elder Miss Wentworth would be more deserving of sympathy, having borne Mrs. Tibbet's company these last few months. Miss Charity Wentworth has only just been introduced to Mrs. Tibbet."

"We're all deserving of sympathy. How we're to endure the next six weeks in that woman's presence without contemplating violence I'm sure I don't know."

"Then you'll be pleased to hear that she's leaving tomorrow morning."

"What? Impossible! She said more than once to me while in town that she intended to escort both Miss Wentworths home after their stay here. Although she used that as an opportunity to make some sly dig to the effect that by that time I might assume that privilege as Miss Wentworth's fiancée!"

"It *was* her intention to stay, it is true, but she changed her mind once she learned of the shortage of rooms here, and that she would be doing me a great favor by delivering a package to your sister in town. Now what do you think I could find to send to Lucy? It has to be of suitable weight so that Mrs. Tibbet could not suspect it could have been delivered some other way. A shawl, perhaps? Some jewelry?"

Sir Anthony laughed and shook his head. "You have vanquished La Tibbet! You are quite formidable, ma'am. I should have applied for you to come to town immediately and I would not have found myself in this predicament. Now, if you can vanquish the young lady while leaving her papa, I will think you the best of mothers."

"You mistake my intentions; I have no desire to vanquish Miss Wentworth, I was taken with her immediately. Such a charming young lady, with an amazing amount of forbearance. I am sure she had need of it when she found herself being courted by you."

"Courted by me? That's a preposterous assertion! Now you sound like Mrs. Tibbet."

"Do I? How alarming. But you will not distract me from a discussion of your own behavior with an attack upon mine. I believe you when you say you were not courting Miss Wentworth—"

"Well, that's a relief—"

"—because you do not have any notion of the meaning of the word."

Sir Anthony opened his mouth to refute this accusation, but then recollecting he had no real desire to court Miss Wentworth, shut it again. His mother had led him into a cunning trap, and he realized she was a much more dangerous foe than Tibbet. Women! They were a wily bunch. How was a mere gentleman ever to compete? They had not the honorable principles of a true sportsman. But he would not be out-gamed by his own mother, b'gad!

Five
ᕍᕓ

Faith was seated between Sir Anthony and Lord Frederick Brand at dinner, and never had she beheld Sir Anthony at such a loss for words. She found herself initiating a conversation about horse racing, just so that she would not have to stare at him as he twirled food around his fork. However, even that attempt fell flat. He did look up with a smile, but his eyes fell upon his mother, seated across from them, and he returned his gaze to his plate after making a monosyllabic reply.

So Faith was forced to speak primarily to Lord Frederick, who was a much more interesting conversationalist than Sir Anthony could ever be. He was inclined to tease her a little, and Faith wondered if he could perhaps be attempting to flirt with her, but she rejected the notion immediately. It was not that she found Lord Frederick in any way undesirable as a suitor, but that she was inclined to get through life by not hoping for too much and her poor heart beat rather too briskly at the thought of Lord Frederick's interest. Far better to dismiss the hope than deal with the inevitable disappointment.

Lord Frederick had overheard her remark to Sir Anthony and was prepared to follow up on it. "Are you a horsewoman then, Miss Wentworth?"

"I do like riding very much, though I don't participate in the hunt. I am afraid I am far too meek and spiritless a creature to enjoy the thought of the kill."

Sir Anthony did look up at that, and his eyes met those of Miss Cherry Wentworth. The condescending expression on both their faces amused Lady Burke immensely. However, Mrs. Tibbet was dominating the conversation on the other side of the table, and even Cherry's strength of personality was subdued by the forceful character of the matchmaker, so she presented as lackluster an appearance at dinner as Sir Anthony.

When it was time for the ladies to leave the gentlemen Sir Anthony could scarce contain his delight, and the ladies heard him calling jovially for the port before the door to the dining room had even closed behind them.

"You will never believe it," Sir Anthony told Lord Frederick, "but it's just as I predicted: my mother is now as determined a matchmaker as the Machiavellian Mrs. Tibbet."

"I would never put your mother in the same category as Mrs. Tibbet."

"Of course not, she's my own mother, after all, but you know how mothers can be unreasonable on this one subject."

"Yes," Lord Frederick replied, as he had gone to town himself at *his* mother's urging.

"She keeps yammering on about Miss Wentworth, finds her charming and all that. It's enough to make one detest the sight of the young lady." Sir Anthony happened to glance over at Lord Frederick at this point and, remembering his friend's sentiments regarding Faith, he quickly begged his pardon.

"Never mind, I've known you long enough to

know you are completely lacking in good taste or sense. However, I cannot complain, since if you possessed either quality you would no doubt be engaged by now to a young lady you do not deserve."

"And you are more deserving a man than I," Sir Anthony riposted.

"Far more deserving. Both my mother and my nanny have assured me many times of my worth."

Sir Anthony grinned, but quickly turned morose once again. "*My* mother tells me I have no notion of how to court a young lady."

"Your mother is very astute. But I hope you don't set about trying to change her opinion of you."

"No, I didn't fall for *that* trick. I was very careful not to let one word that could be mistaken for courtship pass my lips at dinner this evening."

"Nor even any that could be mistaken for a full sentence," Lord Frederick told his friend.

"Now you sound disapproving! How, pray tell, am I to extricate myself from this situation?"

"I've been thinking about that and I've got an idea. If we can somehow appeal to the Captain's sportsmanship, we can distract him from his desire to see his daughter married to you. He's got a reputation, as you know, for never turning down a wager. I believe we could use his game-playing tendencies to our advantage."

"How so?" Sir Anthony asked.

Before Lord Frederick could reply, there was an interruption in the form of the arrival of Captain Wentworth.

He had arrived during dinner but had been escorted to his room to change before joining the company. By the time he arrived downstairs dinner was over, but the purely masculine company that greeted him was far more pleasing to him than a dining room full of squawking females, even if two of the females were his own daughters.

He found himself wholeheartedly welcomed by his host, Sir Anthony, and received not quite as enthusiastically, but very graciously, by Lord Frederick.

Captain Wentworth was one of those rare persons whose presence in person was as outstanding as the reputation that preceded him. He was not extraordinarily tall, standing an inch below six feet, but his muscular forearms and broad shoulders made him an imposing physical presence, and he was as fit at forty-seven as he'd been at twenty. There was no doubt that he was capable of all the feats ascribed to him, and if there were some exaggerations made, as there always are, they were not outside the realm of possibility.

Sir Anthony called a servant to order dinner for his guest, and was quickly overruled by Captain Wentworth. "Only some undercooked beefsteak for me, as close to raw as it can be. And have you any home-brewed ale? I would have brought my own, but I neglected to send it with the carriage and it was more of a burden than I wanted on my walk."

"Of course, of course. Simmons, could you bring some ale and beefsteak for our guest? I would have suggested it myself, Captain, but I didn't realize you were in training."

"I am not training *per se*, but spices are always bad for the constitution, Sir Anthony, and too many courses confuse the internal organs and the food turns rancid in the stomach. What does a horse eat, I ask you? Do they have turbot in sauce and cheeses and minced chicken? No, they have very little variety in their diet, and look how well they perform physically. You would fare far better if you ordered half the food you do for your dinners. You are more than welcome to come to Eaton Park some time and see how we dine there."

If poor Lord Frederick's interest hadn't already been caught by Faith, he would have resolved then and there never to set foot on the Wentworth estate. As it was, he spared a thought for her, and hoped that the ladies had a different menu than their father. Sir Anthony, on the other hand, wondered if he should be taking notes. Captain Wentworth was a fount of knowledge, just as he'd always anticipated he would be.

"Thank you for the invitation, Captain Wentworth, I will be sure to take you up on it," said Sir Anthony. "Perhaps I could even join you in walking there. I am overcome with curiosity: what time did you make? Your daughter tells me you left your estate at four this morning. So I put the time at a little over sixteen hours?"

"Not quite sixteen; you forget that I washed up before dinner. No, it was fifteen and a half."

Lord Frederick was impressed in spite of himself. This man had been walking for over fifteen hours and did not look fatigued in the least. And rather than retire for the evening, he looked as if he were prepared to stay downstairs indefinitely. Lord Frederick began to wonder if the Captain's odd diet did have some benefit. But, even so, it was not enough to tempt him to undertake it.

"If you have some white Lisbon handy I will

have a glass of that while we wait for the ale," Captain Wentworth told his host. "I find it is not too deleterious if drunk in moderate amounts."

Sir Anthony poured the Captain a glass, the Captain observing him closely as he did so. "I hear you are interested in my eldest gel."

Sir Anthony almost spilled the drink, so nervous did this statement make him. He handed the Captain his glass of wine, looking over at Lord Frederick with a panicked expression, before finally remarking nervously, "Charming girls, both your daughters."

"Yes, but I do think Faith is the superior of the two. The younger one is a hard filly to break to bridle," her Papa said, shaking his head in dismay. Sir Anthony looked as if he were about to mount a spirited defense of the younger daughter, who he was beginning to feel was vastly underappreciated by those around her. Before he could do so, Lord Frederick joined the conversation.

"We *both* enjoyed making Miss Wentworth's acquaintance in town."

"Yes, but she can't marry both of you," Captain Wentworth said, laughing heartily at his own wit. "And that Tibbet woman told me Sir Anthony has the inside track."

"It's a little early to say…" Sir Anthony ventured.

"Show some decision, man," the Captain barked at him. "I can't abide such feminine flustering."

There was no sentence better designed to get Sir Anthony to the altar, and Lord Frederick jumped into the conversation before Sir Anthony proposed to Captain Wentworth on the spot.

"I have a proposal for you, Captain," Lord Frederick said with a smile, but the irony of his remark was lost on his hearers, the Captain merely replying, "Go on," and Sir Anthony swallowing nervously. "Marriage is a gamble, as I am sure you will agree. At stake is the future happiness of the participants, the health of their progeny and the family's prosperity. I say we gentlemen make a game of that gamble."

Mention games to a sportsman and one is assured of capturing his attention. "Very novel, Lord Frederick," said the Captain, holding out his glass for a refill. "What is it you propose?"

"You are well-known for expounding the virtues of training for horses and athletes, is that not right? How about training for the role of husband?"

"That's preposterous, young man. Why is it necessary to train? I've never heard such poppycock. Ladies, of course, are trained from birth in the genteel, submissive qualities required, and this is how it should be, as the gentleman is naturally master of his domain and requires no training to behave so."

"I bow to your superior wisdom, Captain," Lord Frederick said, suiting action to word, "but is it not also true that many a marriage founders due to ignorance on the part of its principles? Many a man and woman enter into the wedded state with no more knowledge of each other than the superficial; his or her appearance and property. I suggest that we young men undertake to get to know the likes and dislikes, virtues and faults of the young women in attendance at the house party. The rules of the game are simple: No engagement is permitted to take place unless the young man is able to correctly answer a series of questions posed concerning the nature and habits of his prospective bride. The rules will also apply to Mr. Perrywhistle when he arrives."

"Who is to pose these questions? And how will he know the correct answers?"

"We need a disinterested third party, it's true. What about your vicar, Sir Anthony? Is he a man of sound understanding?"

Sir Anthony looked a little dazed, as if still unrecovered from his narrow escape, but he snapped to attention at last. "Foster? He's quite a good chap. Knew him at school."

"Do you think he could be induced to participate as a sort of superintendent, or referee, of our game?"

"I'm sure of it," Sir Anthony said, resolved to bribe him, if necessary, and determined to get every answer wrong when questioned about Miss Wentworth.

"Good. He will decide upon the questions without our knowledge, and then interview the ladies himself and record their answers. Then he will in turn interview the gentlemen. However, if a gentleman finds upon further discussion with the lady that he is not interested in pursuing the match, he is withdrawn from the competition. Is it necessary to record the rules?" Lord Frederick asked the Captain.

"No, it is not strictly a bet, unless someone wants to make it more interesting," he suggested, trying to devise in his head a way he could marry off his daughters *and* collect a monetary prize. But it was decided by the other two gentlemen present that the Captain would never want to risk jeopardizing his daughters' reputation by betting on such a thing, and the Captain allowed himself to be persuaded he was a better father than he in actuality ever was, or even aspired to be.

Six

❧

The ladies waited in the drawing room while, unbeknownst to them, the gentlemen hammered out the details of the game in which they were soon to become unwitting participants. Lady Burke had been told of the arrival of Captain Wentworth, and had informed the other ladies of his presence, so they all knew he was in the dining room. Faith was a little unnerved that he might be in conversation with Sir Anthony concerning a betrothal that she had no desire to occur, but she had been happily distracted by Lady Burke's question concerning her musical tastes. She discovered that Lady Burke had quite a large collection of music, which she offered to allow Faith to copy while staying at Kenilworth. Faith could think of no better holiday than one that allowed her unrestricted access to a wide variety of literature and music, her two chief interests.

Cherry, of course, found such topics deadly dull, and sat rather sulkily on the sofa, contributing little to the conversation. Mrs. Tibbet's contribution was to tell Cherry to sit up straight, "for no gentleman wants to marry a hunchback." This stricture had no noticeable effect on Cherry's posture or mood, except perhaps to make both worse.

Lady Burke, seeing her guest was uncomfortable, made an effort to draw Cherry into her conversation with Faith. "Miss Charity," she began, in her soft, low voice that made one instinctively draw closer to her.

"Please, my lady," Cherry interrupted, her expression lightening immediately, "call me 'Cherry.' All my intimates call me so."

"But Charity is such a lovely name!" Lady Burke protested.

"Do you think so? I find it sadly ill-suited to me."

"But why? It is the most beautiful word in the English language, as at its root is love."

"I suppose I think more in terms of its association with good works and piety. I don't know, it seems like a stuffy, proper sort of name, while I prefer more active, outdoor pursuits. Cherries are such a merry, shiny sort of fruit."

Faith said nothing about her own contribution to Cherry's dislike of her name, but felt a twinge of guilt when she remembered how she'd teased her about it when they were children.

"If your intimates call you Cherry, I can do no less, can I?" Lady Burke asked. "I would like very much to improve our acquaintance." She smiled kindly at Cherry, and Cherry returned the smile, unconsciously straightening in her seat.

Faith was astounded at the effect Lady Burke was having on Cherry, and wondered at it. She could only assume Cherry had felt the lack of maternal love in their lives as sorely as Faith had. Faith had thought that she was the only one affected, as Cherry seemed to enter into their father's and brother's pursuits so readily, and disdain anything that hinted of femininity. But perhaps that was Cherry's way of coping with the loss of their mother. It made Faith feel more in sympathy with her sister than she ever had before, and she found herself smiling, as well.

Perhaps the only one not included in this communal moment of goodwill was Mrs. Tibbet, who began to wonder if she should go to bed and try to speak to Captain Wentworth in the morning, as it appeared he may never come out of the dining room.

❧

The gentlemen never did join the ladies, and they retired to their rooms without seeing them again that night. Faith, who was well familiar with her father's habits, entered the breakfast room at an unfashionably early hour, to find him harassing the servants into providing him with more beefsteak and ale.

"And have you no stale bread? This bread is far too fresh to digest easily."

"Good morning, Papa," Faith said, moving toward him and bestowing a kiss on his cheek.

"Faith," he exclaimed good-naturedly, "there you are. I wonder if you know where I could find a decent map of this area. I'm inclined to walk thirty miles before dinner and I want to select a circular route."

Faith promised to help him find a map, not at all surprised that her father was totally engrossed in his own concerns. "But, Papa, Mrs. Tibbet is to leave this morning, and she cannot do so until she speaks with you."

"Probably wants to be paid. I'll tell you what: I'll leave you my purse and you can give her the money. Make sure you give her a little something extra. I am very pleased with her; she found you an excellent match in no time at all. Mr. Bellington, who recommended Mrs. Tibbet to me, told me he believed it wouldn't take longer than four months for you to make a match, as it took his girl nine and she had a crossed-eye, but I was tempted to make odds on it taking six months or more. I am glad I did not. I would have lost my shirt."

Faith did not think this the appropriate time to tell her father she had no intention of marrying Sir Anthony, as she wanted nothing to delay Mrs. Tibbet's departure. So she merely took the money from her father and helped him find his map, before wishing him a pleasant walk.

After he departed she returned to her chamber to sleep a little longer. The second time she entered the breakfast room she found all the ladies of the house party were present. There was a general chorus of good mornings and Faith selected something from the sideboard and joined them at the table.

"But, Faith, where is Captain Wentworth this morning?" Mrs. Tibbet asked. "I am prepared to leave after breakfast, as the Marchioness of Trent is expecting me in town, and I would like to speak with him before I do so."

"Unfortunately he has already left for a long walk and will not be returning until late in the day. However, he gave me something to give to you, and asked me to tell you that he is very pleased with your chaperonage of me."

"I see. That is good news, of course. I did want to give him more of the details of our season in town, but I suppose I can trust you to do so." Mrs. Tibbet

looked uncertainly at Faith as she said this, as she knew
Faith to be resistant to the match with Sir Anthony, but
since it appeared she herself would be paid whether the
match took place or not, she quickly decided it was in
her best interests to be paid sooner rather than later.

"Yes, ma'am, you can trust me to tell my father
all that it is necessary for him to know," Faith said, the
picture of submissive obedience.

They retired to the drawing room after breakfast,
where Faith gave Mrs. Tibbet her *doucer* and made a
very civil, if not entirely sincere, expression of thanks for
Mrs. Tibbet's role in introducing her to London society.
Mrs. Tibbet was so overcome by the receipt of the
money that she took Faith's hand very tenderly, her protuberant blue eyes a little more watery than usual, and
said, "I must give credit where credit is due, and tell you
that it was not due to my efforts alone that you are now
so well established. Certainly some of the credit must go
to you for your compliance with my guidance."

Since this was merely a back-handed compliment
to Mrs. Tibbet herself, and thus was no compliment at
all, Faith just nodded in response, removed her hand
from Mrs. Tibbet's grasp, and wished her a pleasant
journey.

"Thank you, my dear. And when I return to Kenilworth sometime in the future and you are mistress of
this establishment, you will not hear any vulgar 'I told
you so' from my lips. No, I am not the kind of person
to crow over my successes, but rather I delight only in
seeing the happiness of my charges when they take on
the roles for which nature designed them."

Faith was glad Lady Burke entered the drawing

room at that point, intent on seeing Mrs. Tibbet on her way, for she could see Mrs. Tibbet was in no hurry to leave when given an opportunity to sing her own praises. Thankfully, Lady Burke took her guest in hand and soon was escorting her to the door, without Mrs. Tibbet becoming at all aware that she was being firmly ejected from the premises.

Having finally dispensed with her unwanted guest, Lady Burke returned with Faith to the drawing room.

"My dear, where is your sister this morning?"

"I am not sure, Lady Burke. I believe she probably went for a walk. It is her habit to do so every day."

"And you do not have a similar habit?"

"I do, but I must admit I do not walk in the same manner my father and sister do. When they walk they view it as a sport, and are conscious at all times of their form, and the rate of their steps, and their level of endurance. I walk more in the manner of a poet, I think," Faith said, a twinkle in her eye.

"I am unfamiliar with the walking habits of poets, my dear. Do they have a certain stride they favor?"

Faith laughed. "No, my lady, not to my knowledge. It is just I have read that the poets of the Lake District take walks to feed their muse, to gain inspiration, and to appreciate the wondrous beauties of nature. I am not a poet but, like them, I'd rather nourish my soul than my body."

"I agree with you, my dear. Sports are well and good in their place, but the spiritual is always of higher value than the physical. But if you are in the habit of walking, why did you not walk today?"

"I can walk any time, but I do not always have access to such a collection of music as you possess. I was hoping you would allow me to begin copying some of the pieces."

"Of course, dear child, of course! I must admit that I seldom play these days, so if you would learn a few of the pieces and play them for me you would be doing me a great favor. I miss my daughters' playing."

So Faith soon found herself happily picking out tunes on the pianoforte, oblivious to time or place, as she struggled to learn a piece by Clementi. Once she had tired of practicing, she began playing a Welsh song she'd learned in London, singing as she did so:

Oh let the night my blushes hide,
Whilst thus my sighs reveal,
What modest love and maiden pride
Forever would conceal.
What can he mean, how can he bear,
Thus falt'ring to delay;
How can his eyes, his eyes so much declare,
His tongue so little say, his tongue so little say?

Faith had a pretty voice, perhaps not strong enough if one was disposed to be critical, but sweet and true. And Lord Frederick, passing by the room at that moment, was not at all a harsh critic.

He carefully opened the door and shut it again behind him, not wishing to interrupt her performance. He was able to observe her for a minute or two, but far sooner than he wished she seemed to sense his presence and her hands stilled at the keyboard. She looked over at him, having just sung the end of the second stanza:

But must we wait till age and care
Shall fix our wedding day;
How can his eyes so much declare,
His tongue so little say?

Had Lord Frederick known how much his eyes declared at that moment, he would have glanced away, as Faith had no darkness in which to hide her blushes.

"Lord Frederick," she said, rising from her seat in confusion, "you startled me."

He could tell she was embarrassed, and assumed she was unused to performing before an audience. "I apologize, that was not my desire. You sounded lovely. Pray, continue."

"Oh, no, I could not. I have played far too long as it is." She looked over at the mantel clock, and seemed surprised at the time. "Why, it is almost time for luncheon."

"Yes, that is why I returned to the house. I was riding with Sir Anthony. We met your father and sister on our ride, though separately."

"Yes, they were both out walking, I believe."

"Did you not wish to join them?"

"No, not today, when Lady Burke was kind enough to share some of her sheet music with me."

"You are quite fond of music, are you not? The first time I ever saw you was at Lady Hartley's musicale."

"Yes," Faith said, staring at him in wonder at his remembering such an insignificant event amidst the busy London season. "I did attend Lady Hartley's musicale.

But, I am sorry, I do not recall meeting you there."

"You did not meet me there. We were unacquainted at the time, much to my dismay."

Faith found herself blushing again, and almost wished someone would come and interrupt their *tête-à-tête*. Lord Frederick was blocking her exit, as he stood with his back to the door, and she was unsure if it was proper for them to be alone together. She also felt that the song she had been singing had created an atmosphere that was both heady and dangerous, and one with which she had no prior experience. The way Lord Frederick had looked at her in the past, and looked at her now, was alarming in its intensity. She began to wonder if she were altogether right to despise Sir Anthony's innocuous presence. *He* had only bored her, not made her feel like this. She couldn't even describe what it was she felt, though she knew that she was far from bored, and not at all comfortable.

Lord Frederick left his post by the door, and walked further into the room. This was even more alarming, as he stopped within a few inches of where Faith stood. "Miss Wentworth, do you not wonder why I remember seeing you at the musicale?" he asked her.

"I hope I did not draw attention to myself in some vulgar way," Faith said. To her dismay, she found herself breathing a little too rapidly. She hoped Lord Frederick would not notice.

"On the contrary. You were—"

Before Lord Frederick could finish his sentence, the door to the drawing room began to open. Lord Frederick leapt back in surprise, and Faith turned toward the pianoforte, nervously rearranging the sheets of music that were spread out. She really had no idea what to do and felt extremely foolish. Lord Frederick should not have shut the door. It gave their meeting an appearance of impropriety.

She looked up to see who was entering the room, and found her hostess there, a slight wrinkle between her brow.

"Good afternoon Miss Wentworth, Lord Frederick. You have come down early for luncheon, I see."

"Yes," replied Lord Frederick, as Faith said, "No!" a little too loudly. They looked at each other and then Faith began again, "That is, Lord Frederick came down for luncheon; I was playing the pianoforte when he arrived. It was not more than five minutes ago, isn't that right, Lord Frederick?"

"I apologize, I neglected to check the time," Lord Frederick said, beginning to look amused. Faith wished she possessed a little of his sang-froid. She tried to appear as unconcerned as he, and dropped a sheet of music on the floor.

"Oh, how clumsy of me," she said, bending down to retrieve it. She was not fast enough, and Lord Frederick handed it to her, reading the title aloud as he did so.

"'Oh let the night my blushes hide.' A pretty song, do you not agree, Lady Burke?"

"Very pretty," she said, but gave Lord Frederick a stern look, before turning to Faith with a smile. "Come, my dear, sit down next to me and tell me what other songs you've been playing this morning."

Faith did as Lady Burke suggested, and Lord Frederick sat as well, but Faith was still conscious of him staring at her, a slight smile on his lips, and she wished he would not discompose her so. She could barely attend to her conversation with Lady Burke.

However, there was soon a diversion in the form of the arrival of the Perrywhistle party, and Faith was able to regain her composure.

The Perrywhistles were a family of four: Mrs. Perrywhistle, a widow, and her three children. They lived in a neighboring county and Mr. Perrywhistle was Lady Burke's cousin. The family had been in town for the season so Faith had seen them there, but they had not been introduced. Mr. James Perrywhistle was the eldest, the second child was Miss Diana Perrywhistle, an elegant young lady of two and twenty, and the third Miss Lydia Perrywhistle, who had just turned sixteen.

Charity had entered the drawing room in time for the introductions, and Miss Perrywhistle, who had taken a seat next to Lord Frederick, said, "I have never before regretted my Christian name, but now, Mama, I begin to think you should have named the two of us girls Hope and Prudence, and we could have had all the virtues represented."

Lord Frederick smiled at Miss Perrywhistle's joke, but Faith did not find the remark at all funny. However, she was unsure if it was the joke that annoyed her or Miss Perrywhistle, who continued to smile in Lord Frederick's direction.

"Miss Taylor's Christian name is Felicity," ventured Miss Lydia Perrywhistle, gesturing toward her governess. The poor governess looked appalled at being made the focus of attention, and whispered something about a good name being better than precious ointment.

"Her papa was a rector," Miss Lydia said, in explanation of her governess's obscure biblical quote.

"Who holds the living at Kenilworth now that Mr. Alistair has passed?" Mrs. Perrywhistle asked Lady Burke, and Faith ignored the ensuing conversation as she turned her attention to the elder Miss Perrywhistle.

Miss Perrywhistle was judged by all of her acquaintance as a very pretty girl, but this was more because of her air than because of any outstanding natural endowments she possessed. She was not ill-favored, but her eyes were a trifle small for true beauty and her complexion and hair too pale. Still, her figure was good and she dressed so well and projected such an air of confidence that one overlooked any deficiencies in her appearance immediately, and thought her almost as good-looking as she thought herself.

Faith had hoped to find her a sympathetic companion and had looked forward to making her acquaintance, but she found instead that Miss Perrywhistle's confident manner made her feel even more awkward and unsure of herself. She supposed it was a result of Miss Perrywhistle being a few years older and more at ease in society. Faith's isolated life in the country, compounded by her less-than-successful London season, had resulted in a tendency toward shyness. Perhaps that was why Lord Frederick's friendly attention had made her uncomfortable. She glanced in his direction, resolving to meet his gaze if he was once again looking her way. Unfortunately, he had just addressed a remark to Miss Perrywhistle and was paying no heed to Faith at all.

Seven

❧❦❧

While the ladies made their toilettes for dinner,
the gentlemen retired to the billiards room. The Captain
had skipped luncheon but had arrived back at the house
in time to partake very happily in the billiards game,
quickly potting eight balls and winning the pool. He felt
that there was time for a second game before dinner, but
Lord Frederick, not inclined to lose any more money
that evening, told him that it was time Mr. Perrywhistle
was informed of the game of marital stakes in progress.

Once informed of the particulars Mr. Perrywhistle, seeing a way to relieve some of the boredom he normally felt in a drawing room, said he would be delighted
to take part in it. "Who are the contenders?" he asked.
"I'm not quite ready to tie the knot, but any man can
prepare for the future, what?"

"You've met them," Lord Frederick told him.
"The Misses Wentworths and now your lovely sisters
are included, of course."

"I can't court my own sisters, and there are only
two other females in residence. Seems like I've been
given very poor odds. Besides, you've already had a day
to scout the field. I must say, I don't think that's very
sporting of you."

"There are other ladies in the vicinity, are there
not?" Lord Frederick asked Sir Anthony.

"Of course there are, more young ladies than you can shake a stick at. Can't recall their names at the moment," he said, his brow furrowing as he strove to remember even one eligible female. Finally, excited that he'd thought of one, he said a little too enthusiastically, "The vicar's sister, Miss Foster, is a stunner." Then, realizing the Captain might not appreciate him praising another young woman when he was ostensibly courting his daughter, he hurried to add, "Or so I've heard. Can't say I've noticed particularly myself. Might have brown hair. Could be blonde. She does have hair, at any rate."

"That's a relief," Lord Frederick said, giving Sir Anthony a quizzical look. "I think courting a hairless woman is against the rules."

"Nonsense, there's no specific rule against it," the Captain interjected, and there was a slight pause, before Lord Frederick suggested Sir Anthony invite the vicar and his sister to dinner tomorrow.

"I'd be happy to. I could ask my mother if she knows of any other young ladies who might like to come, as well," Sir Anthony said, beginning to think Lord Frederick's plan might just have a chance of succeeding. If Lord Frederick didn't marry Miss Wentworth, here was Mr. Perrywhistle wanting a crack at her, and perhaps the Vicar could be encouraged to take her in to dinner. At any rate, with so many players on the field, it wouldn't be so obvious if he slowly withdrew himself from the fray.

"I have a question," Mr. Perrywhistle said, interrupting Sir Anthony's thoughts. "If a gentleman passes the test, but does not want to make a match with the young lady, is there a prize of equal value? As I mentioned, I have no intention of marrying at this time, and it hardly seems worthwhile for me to join the game if there's nothing in it for me. And even if one of us did pass the test and want to marry the young lady, the young lady could refuse us, also resulting in no prize being awarded."

"Good point, Perrywhistle. How about £20 to the gentleman who succeeds in answering all the questions correctly, even if he does not become affianced? As it is not actually a bet, but more in the nature of an award, I do not think it is improper. I will put up the stake myself," Lord Frederick said, hoping his friend appreciated the lengths to which he was going to save him from his own folly.

"That's a small stake," Sir Anthony complained. "Isn't there a proverb that says a virtuous woman is worth more than rubies? Tell you what, Foster's a vicar, he'll know the quote I'm referring to."

Lord Frederick glared at his friend. "If you have some rubies you'd like to donate I'm sure none of us would complain."

"No, no, your idea is a good one. £20 for answering some questions correctly is more than generous. I will go by and see Foster in the morning and tell him he's been appointed superintendent."

"Maybe I'll go with you," Mr. Perrywhistle said. "I don't want you getting the inside track with another young lady. Besides, I'd like to see Miss Foster on her home turf."

Lord Frederick began to think perhaps putting dedicated gamesters on the trail of a bevy of unsuspecting ladies might not be as brilliant an idea as he'd first thought, but it was too late for doubts now. Let the games begin!

❧

When the party gathered in the drawing room before dinner Mr. Perrywhistle, to Lord Frederick's dismay, latched onto Faith and began interrogating her. Lord Frederick stood within hearing range, curious what his questions and her answers would be. He supposed he should have realized that Perrywhistle would have little choice but to woo Faith, when the other ladies in the house were either related to him, or too old or too young. And, of course, Faith would still be tempting were there a dozen eligible young misses to choose from.

She took the interrogation in good humor, asking Mr. Perrywhistle some questions of her own. He answered briefly and then excused himself. Lord Frederick watched him walk to a desk in the corner and jot down some notes. It appeared he had more interest in the game than the lady, and Lord Frederick hoped things would remain that way. Before Lord Frederick could speak to Faith himself, there was an interruption in the form of the entrance of young Miss Lydia Perrywhistle.

As she had just turned sixteen and would have her debut in town next year, her mother and Lady Burke had agreed that this house party would be a good occasion for her to come out in adult society. So she had put up her hair and was joining them for dinner that evening. Lord Frederick and Faith had to smile as she entered the room, her excitement was so palpable.

"Good evening, I hope I did not keep everyone

waiting," she said, putting her hand up to her hair as if to verify her coiffure was still intact.

"No, not at all. You look lovely," Lady Burke told her. And Lydia did look quite attractive. While she did not make as elegant and confident appearance as her older sister, she radiated good health and humor, her cheeks flushed and rosy. Sir Anthony, well aware that this was in the nature of Lydia's debut, immediately tried to set her at ease, telling her what a delightful gown she was wearing. Her cheeks rosier than ever, she thanked him.

"Mama bought it for me in town," she said, then blushed again. "Though I suppose that is non-consequential. Should I have remarked on your apparel? It is very elegant, indeed."

She looked to her older sister for help, who chuckled good-humoredly, and told her it was unnecessary for her to compliment the gentlemen. "For they are already too full of their own consequence," she said, with a teasing look at Lord Frederick.

"Perhaps it's not necessary, but a compliment is always appreciated," Sir Anthony said, with a smile. Faith found herself liking him more than she ever had in the past, as this was a side of him she had not seen previously. Cherry, however, was finding the entire tableau more than a little irritating.

"Such a to-do over nothing. You would think she was a filly entering the Newmarket Derby," she whispered to her sister, a little too loudly. While the others might not have been able to hear her exact words, it was obvious from her tone that it was in the nature of a complaint. Both the Captain and Sir Anthony frowned at her, and only Cherry knew whose disapproval affected her more. It was apparent from the way she hung her head that she had noted their displeasure and was dismayed by it. Faith, who knew her sister found the frivolity of the social season tedious and the etiquette unimportant, hoped this would be an important lesson for her, even though she did hate for her to have to feel the sting of public humiliation.

"Anthony," Lady Burke said, into the awkward silence that had fallen, "perhaps you could take Lydia into dinner this evening. Captain Wentworth, if you could escort Mrs. Perrywhistle. Mr. Perrywhistle, perhaps you could escort both the Misses Wentworth, and Lord Frederick, you could escort Miss Perrywhistle."

Lord Frederick was not entirely pleased with this arrangement, though he did not make his feelings obvious. He hoped that Faith would be seated on his other side, but was disappointed when entering the dining room to find he was seated between Lady Burke and Miss Perrywhistle, while Faith was seated between Sir Anthony and Mr. Perrywhistle.

Faith, too, did not find the seating arrangement to her liking. She had noticed the lessening of Sir Anthony's attention with a great deal of relief, and hated to be seated at his side once again. However, Mr. Perrywhistle was so eager to talk to her that most of the meal passed without her exchanging one word with Sir Anthony.

Faith was confused by Mr. Perrywhistle's behavior toward her. He appeared extremely interested in her background, habits, and partialities, but she did not feel he was particularly interested in *her*. She wondered if perhaps the poor young man was shy, and had trained himself to converse with others by asking them questions. Still, she probably would have noticed nothing unusual about his manner of conversation if it weren't for his odd habit of repeating some of her answers.

"So you say you were educated at home," Mr. Perrywhistle said, "by a governess with the name of…"

"Biddleton."

"A Miss Biddleton, rhymes with Wimbledon," Mr. Perrywhistle said, under his breath. Faith did not know if he expected her to reply or not. But after he said a second time, "Biddleton rhymes with Wimbledon" she felt some comment was called for. "Actually, perhaps Middleton is a better rhyme. I believe she was from a town not too far from there."

Mr. Perrywhistle seemed much struck by this observation. "Miss Biddleton was from Middleton!" he said. "Miss Biddleton was from Middleton!"

She had no idea why the sentence afforded him so much pleasure and began to wonder if he were perhaps simpleminded. She was actually relieved when Sir Anthony finally addressed her, and she was forced to turn and speak to him.

Sir Anthony was very pleased by the interest Mr. Perrywhistle was paying his dinner companion and would not have spoken to Miss Wentworth at all if it were not for the glare he intercepted from the Captain. It had become obvious that Mr. Perrywhistle was off to a flying start, and now it appeared the Captain expected Sir Anthony to make a come-from-behind win. He supposed he could deflect the Captain's suspicions if he appeared to be taking some part in the game, so he dutifully posed a question to Miss Wentworth.

"Are you fond of any games, Miss Wentworth?"

"I enjoy chess, Sir Anthony," Faith replied, thinking there was no end to the questions she had answered this evening.

"Do you?" Sir Anthony asked, thinking chess a dull game. "Perhaps we could play sometime."

"That would be nice. However, I must warn you I am quite skilled, so under no conditions could I accept a wager on the outcome of our match," Faith said, an expression of mock seriousness on her face. She knew it was not nice to tease Sir Anthony in such a manner, but sporting gentlemen were so easy to bait.

"Nonsense, it is very kind of you to warn me, but I think a small stake would be perfectly acceptable," Sir Anthony replied, who felt no game was dull if there was a bet involved.

"Do you think so? Let me see, what stake should we play for?" she asked, a thoughtful expression on her face, while Sir Anthony waited anxiously for her response. Lord Frederick, who was observing Faith's conversation with his friend, wondered what the deuce Sir Anthony was doing. All of a sudden he was hanging eagerly on Miss Wentworth's every word. But Miss Perrywhistle addressed him and he was forced to turn away from the infuriating sight of his friend behaving as stupidly here as he had in town.

"If I win then you are to have dancing tonight after dinner, and ask my sister and Miss Lydia Perrywhistle to partner you," Faith finally replied, and Sir Anthony felt he had already won a victory, as the poor girl obviously had no idea how to make a bet.

"And if I win?" Sir Anthony asked, thinking if his prize were as paltry as hers perhaps he should just cancel the whole thing.

"If you win then I will share with you one of my father's secret training techniques," Faith told him, and Sir Anthony was beside himself with excitement. When his mother announced it was time for the ladies to leave the gentlemen to their port, Sir Anthony, for the first time in his life, was inclined to dispense with the gentlemanly privilege altogether. However, when he considered the other gentlemen's likely response to such a deviation from accepted behavior he decided against it, though he resolved to hurry them into the drawing room as quickly as possible.

❧

In the drawing room the young ladies eyed each other warily. Faith was inclined to dislike Miss Perrywhistle, as she seemed to feel herself superior to her company, and Miss Lydia Perrywhistle was inclined to dislike Miss Cherry Wentworth for the same reason.

Faith, who did like the younger Miss Perrywhistle, asked Cherry to accompany her over to the pianoforte, ostensibly to show her some of the music, but in reality to tell her out of the others' hearing that she must apologize to Lydia immediately.

"What! Why? You must admit she was causing a great deal of commotion over putting up her hair and sitting down at a table to eat. It was ridiculous. As if any of that matters," Cherry said disdainfully.

"It matters to Lydia Perrywhistle, and to other

young ladies her age. Just because you do not feel a similar interest does not mean it's unimportant. What if she showed such scorn for your interests?"

"I would not care. It does not matter to me what other people think."

"Does it not? I don't believe you. You seemed as if you cared that Papa and Sir Anthony disapproved of your actions." Reminded of that moment, Cherry flushed again. Faith continued, "Do you think Lady Burke would ever treat someone in such a disdainful manner, just because that person's interests differed from her own?"

"No," Cherry said, grudgingly.

"And Cherry, have you ever thought that your interests were formed primarily due to the influence of our father and brothers, and that you could find other things almost as interesting were you to spend time in the company of people with different interests?"

"That's ridiculous. I will never like such silly things most females like, and you can never make me."

"Fine, that is your choice. But neither should you despise other people because they make a choice different from yours. Miss Lydia is a very nice girl, and no one else, not even a sporting gentleman like Sir Anthony, thinks badly of her because she is excited at the prospect of her debut. In fact, a gentleman of the *ton* would only approve of a young lady taking an interest in her appearance."

Cherry looked over at Miss Lydia, who was dressed very fashionably, and then down at her own clothes, which did not fare well in comparison. "But none of that should matter," she said, her gaze pleading with her sister.

"It shouldn't matter, much," Faith agreed, "but it does matter. Just think, Cherry, if appearance did not matter, why are horses groomed and gardens tended? We do judge people by outward appearances, at least prior to finding what their insides might be. Of course, the inside is much more important, but a neat and attractive appearance is a sign of respect for ourselves and others. And it can be such *fun*. For example, what if I told you that when you wear blue your complexion appears brighter and your eyes sparkle like sapphires?"

"That's nonsense," Cherry said, but she couldn't completely hide her pleasure at the compliment.

"We can discuss it later if you'd like, but for now I do think you should speak to Lydia."

Cherry sighed, but nodded, and Faith congratulated herself that she had finally succeeded in reaching her sister. Though she suspected her words would not have had any weight at all were Cherry not infatuated with Sir Anthony.

ॐॐ

Lydia, who really was a good-hearted girl, accepted Cherry's apology gracefully, and the two were soon making attempts to become friends. As Lydia was a keen horsewoman, she and Cherry finally hit on a subject of interest to both of them, and they promised to go riding together as soon as it could be arranged.

Their two older sisters could not be said to enter into a similar harmony with each other, but they both smiled agreeably to see their younger sisters getting along so well, and the atmosphere in the drawing room had brightened considerably by the time the gentlemen rejoined the ladies.

It was rather awkward when all three of the young gentlemen hurried to Faith's side, and Diana Perrywhistle could not remember a time when she had been so neglected in favor of one who, while pretty enough, had no presence and barely any conversation. Diana, for the first time in her life, felt what other young ladies must have felt when they were ignored in *her* favor, and she did not find it at all a comfortable feeling. But there was something quite peculiar about her brother's attentions, at least, as she had never known him to have an interest in any young lady. She had also overheard his very odd rhyme regarding Miss Wentworth's governess at dinner and as she knew, unlike Faith, that her brother was no simpleton, she realized he had been trying to commit the name to memory for some reason. She resolved to discover that reason as soon as possible. In the meantime, Lady Burke was asking her to perform for the company and Diana gratefully acceded to her request. She knew herself to be quite skilled as a musician and she hoped Lord Frederick, who was known to be a gentleman of good taste, would notice.

Diana wasn't quite sure that she wanted to marry Lord Frederick, but she wasn't averse to the idea, either. He was, after all, very attractive, and it was well-known that his older brother, the Marquess of Darby, who had been married ten years at least, had no issue. As the next in line it was highly possible that Lord Frederick would attain the title and estate. However, even if he did not, he was comfortably settled and an extremely desirable *parti* in his own right. A girl could hardly do better than Lord Frederick, and Diana had been excited to know he would be present at Sir Anthony's house party.

And then there was Sir Anthony. Diana had known him all her life, so he did not have the unique appeal that Lord Frederick did, but she had always felt he was hers for the taking should no one better come along. However, as she observed him playing chess with Miss Wentworth, a game she knew he despised, she wondered if she should be so confident.

കൈൽ

Faith had not lied about her skill at chess. She could have won the match in no time at all but, sensitive to Sir Anthony's feelings, she drew it out a few minutes longer. Still, it was barely ten minutes after they began their game that she was saying, "Checkmate."

Sir Anthony couldn't believe his bad luck and was tempted to ask for a re-match, but he really did despise chess and actually enjoyed dancing, so comforted himself with the thought that he could discover the Captain's secrets himself during the course of the house party. He also knew his young cousin would be excited that her first evening in society would culminate in a dance. So he interrupted Miss Perrywhistle's virtuoso performance on the pianoforte to request she play something else.

"Do you know any dances?" he asked her, and she suffered her second affront of the evening. That she, a nubile lady of twenty-two, could be asked to sit at the pianoforte and play while other ladies danced, was an egregious insult to which she hardly knew how to respond. Thankfully, her mother was aware of her daughter's feelings and volunteered at once to play, saying, "My daughter belongs with the dancers, Anthony, as I'm sure you're well aware."

"Of course, Aunt, beg pardon," he said, turning at once to where Miss Lydia sat with Miss Cherry. Both girls looked hopefully at him, and he hated to disappoint either of them, but Lydia was his cousin, and it was her special night. He would dance with Miss Cherry next. However, when he took Lydia's hand, Cherry fought valiantly to hide her disappointment.

Lord Frederick noticed this byplay, and though his inclination was to ask Faith to dance, Cherry's crushed look was more than he could bear, and he presented himself to her as a partner. She eagerly accepted him, and he was rewarded by the huge smile of thanks Faith directed at him, before joining the set herself with Mr. Perrywhistle. Captain Wentworth presented himself to Miss Perrywhistle as a partner, and she was spared the dreadful prospect of sitting out a dance.

However, one of the young ladies was forced to sit out later that evening when the Captain surprised everyone by asking his hostess, Lady Burke, to dance with him.

"That is very kind of you, Captain, but I put up my dancing slippers years ago, I'm afraid," Lady Burke said, though it was an incongruous statement coming from her lips, when she was nearly the same age as the Captain and looked ten years younger.

"My dear lady, if you do not dance I must sit down as well, because I believe I am older than you," the

Captain told her.

When the other ladies also urged her to dance, she laughingly complied, and Faith observed her father and Lady Burke speculatively. She had thought as a young child that it might be nice to acquire a step-mama, but when the years passed and her father demonstrated no desire to remarry, she was not too disappointed. A step-mother could just as easily be a curse as a blessing. But if Lady Burke were to become her step-mother, that would be a blessing indeed!

Lord Frederick noticed that Faith was closely observing Lady Burke, and as she also spent much of her time that evening watching Sir Anthony, he started to worry that she was not as averse to Sir Anthony's suit as he'd previously assumed. And, according to Sir Anthony, Lady Burke was as eager to see him married to Faith as Captain Wentworth was, so it would be even more difficult for Faith to resist, especially as she appeared to admire Lady Burke. Lord Frederick had little notion that Faith was wondering if perhaps Sir Anthony and Cherry might make a match of it, which would also bring Lady Burke into the family. Faith strongly suspected her sister was already attracted to Sir Anthony and, as Cherry and Sir Anthony shared so many interests, Faith felt they were much better suited than she and Sir Anthony were, but she did not know if an interest in sports was enough to sustain them throughout their married life. However, if Lady Burke were to take Cherry under her wing she could perhaps interest her in other, more worthwhile pursuits, and train her in the behavior necessary to perform her duties as the wife of a Baronet.

When the dancing was over and Supper was

served Lord Frederick found a seat next to Faith and noticed she was again looking in Lady Burke's direction.

"I have a mother, too, you know," he told her.

Faith was not entirely sure she knew what this conversational gambit implied, though she had her suspicions. "Do you? Most people do, at one time or another," she said.

"And my mother would find you as charming as Lady Burke does."

"It is kind of you to say so."

"I am not being kind; I am merely pointing out that just because you like Lady Burke, and may even desire to have a closer connection with her, that is no reason to rush into a relationship that may not suit."

"Do not worry; I am not given to rash judgments," she said, finally certain she understood his meaning and feeling her heart race at its implications. She paid little attention to Sir Anthony or Lady Burke the rest of the evening, finding that Lord Frederick's company and conversation fully captured her interest.

Eight

ತಾ⊶ஓ

When Cherry came to Faith's room before bed
that night to ask if she might use a little of her Crème de
L'Enclos to lighten her complexion, Faith could hardly
believe her ears. Was her little sister finally acknowledg-
ing that she was a lady, and not a boy in skirts? But the
next morning, she felt she'd begun celebrating a little
early.

At the breakfast table Cherry asked Faith to give
her excuses to Lydia, who had not yet joined them. "For
I shan't be able to go riding with her, as Sir Anthony has
a mare foaling and I'd like to be there for the birth."

Faith looked in dismay at Lady Burke, the only
other person at the table, sure she'd be disgusted at her
sister's unladylike behavior. Lady Burke's expression
gave nothing away, but in her embarrassment Faith said a
little more harshly than usual, "Cherry, please, show
some decorum. It is not acceptable for you to be hanging around the stables in the company of men. You will
go riding with Lydia, as you promised."

"Why must you always tell me what to do? You
are not my mother, you know. At times, I wish you were
not even my sister," Cherry said, before getting up and
stomping from the room.

"I beg your pardon, Lady Burke," Faith said.
"We must seem very ill-bred. I am not sure why my sis-

ter must act in such an unladylike manner."

"I was not shocked, I assure you. I have visited the stables more than once myself. Perhaps you expect too much from your sister, and yourself," Lady Burke told her, very gently, to remove the sting from her words.

"I just want her to display behavior more fitting for a lady. You see, our mother died when we were both very young, and the only model for behavior she's had has been masculine. I think she forgets she's a young lady."

"I think you forget, as well."

"What do you mean?" Faith asked, genuinely confused.

"You take yourself so *seriously*, my dear. 'Tis true that you can provide an example for your younger sister, but you are not her mother, as she rightly pointed out. Your father has put too much of a burden upon you, expecting you to be responsible for your younger sister's behavior at the expense of your own youth. Cherry is too inclined to be frivolous in her pursuit of games and sport but, if you ask me, you're not frivolous enough."

Faith was silent for a moment, digesting this statement. She wondered if she appeared self-righteous and priggish to the rest of the house party. It was an embarrassing thought. She was grateful when Lady Burke came to sit beside her, taking her hand. "Dear Faith, now you're frowning more than ever. I did not mean to further dampen your spirits, but to encourage you to enjoy yourself and not to worry so much about Cherry. The more time she spends in polite company the more she will be able to judge for herself what her behavior should be. She is still young, and not beyond reform at seventeen. But you must live your own life, my dear, and not constitute yourself your sister's chaperon when you are only twenty."

Faith was still embarrassed, but managed to smile at Lady Burke. "That is good advice, Lady Burke. I will try to focus more on my own behavior, rather than my sister's. I do not remember my mother very well, either, so I suppose my conduct, too, suffers from the lack of a proper role model."

"Faith, you are a young lady to make any mother proud," Lady Burke told her, and Faith felt a little better. So she made her goodbyes to Lady Burke and went upstairs in search of her sister.

She knocked on the door of Cherry's room and entered quickly, finding her sitting glumly in front of the mirror. "Did you want to lecture me some more?" Cherry asked Faith, turning away from her image.

"No, I wanted to apologize, and ask you if you might like company in the stables," Faith told her.

Cherry looked shocked. "What did you say?"

"I must apologize, Cherry. Last night I told you that a real lady doesn't show disdain if another's interests do not match her own. I must have sounded like a hypocrite to you, as I am often disdainful of your interest in sporting pursuits." There was a pause, but Cherry did not reply, so Faith continued, "I told you I thought you were unnaturally influenced by our father and brothers, but I must admit I, too, have been influenced, but in the opposite manner you were. I hope that I can join you on your excursion, and that you'll forgive me for being overly critical of your behavior."

Cherry wasn't the sort to throw herself weeping onto her sister's breast, or to show much emotion at all. If Faith had hoped for a moving scene of reconciliation she would have hoped in vain. Cherry merely nodded and suggested Faith change her morning gown into something more suitable for the stables.

When they finally did arrive at the stables, Faith was surprised to find nearly the entire house party there, including both Misses Perrywhistle. Cherry heroically refrained from commenting on the presence of the young ladies but she was not so mature she couldn't resist a sarcastic look at her older sister. The mare had already dropped the foal, and it was standing on rickety, uncertain legs peering up at them. Faith was feeling herself foolish indeed to forbid Cherry such an outing, as she immediately fell in love with the little foal and was glad that her ridiculous notions of propriety hadn't kept her from such an enchanting sight.

After an appropriate amount of ooh-ing and ah-ing had passed, Sir Anthony mentioned he had an appointment in town with the Vicar.

"Don't forget you said I could accompany you," said Mr. Perrywhistle, causing his sister to look at him like he'd grown another head.

"You're full of surprises lately, James," Diana said to him softly, and her brother found himself avoiding her narrow-eyed gaze. Dash it, she was much too quick on the intake, that sister of his.

"Would you ladies care to join us on a walk into the village?" Sir Anthony asked, as he had been reminded that morning by his mother that this house party had been his idea, and he should bestir himself to entertain his guests. Unfortunately, the only guest he really wanted to entertain was the Captain, who insisted on disappearing every morning before Anthony had even awoken. But since it was already necessary for him to go to the village, there was no harm in the young ladies accompanying him there. And as he had an appointment with the vicar, he had a perfect excuse to avoid accompanying them to the shops, something that gave him a shudder to contemplate.

Poor Lord Frederick had no such excuse, and might find himself having to offer his opinion on ribbons or, God forbid, bonnets, but he manfully hid his disappointment. If Sir Anthony were to ask him, Frederick would have admitted his only disappointment was in his lack of success at courting Faith. He had no clue when he started this silly game that James Perrywhistle would be so irritatingly dogged in his pursuit of Faith, and that Miss Perrywhistle would be so dogged in her pursuit of *him.*

He had felt his interest in Faith heighten since they arrived at Kenilworth, in spite of the fact that she seemed more reserved with him here than she had in town, and he hoped he was not one of those fickle gentlemen who only wanted what he could not have. Another reason he had for questioning his character was because he'd found himself attracted to Diana Perrywhistle on past occasions, but now that she seemed intent on monopolizing his attention he was totally unmoved by her sparkling looks and flirtatious ways.

He was not, at twenty-five, in a particular hurry to get married, but his mother had been very disappointed that his older brother had thus far failed to give

her any grandchildren, so he'd promised her to take a serious look about him when he went to town. When he
did so, he'd found that Faith was the only one who made
him take a second look. She was not so vivacious as
Diana, but he had observed that Faith was a little shy,
and he found himself thinking that not a bad quality at
all. Faith would not flirt indiscriminately with any gentleman of fortune, but if she did find herself in love,
would let her guard down with the young man who possessed her heart. He was hopeful he would be that man.
But when Mr. Perrywhistle skirted passed him to give his
arm to Faith on the walk to town, he realized he needed
to step up his game if he were to win the prize.

❧

Unaware that Lord Frederick had just decided
how pleased he was that she was shy, Faith made every
effort to act in a more gregarious manner than she had in
the past. She felt the truth of Lady Burke's comment
that she was too serious, so she was determined to laugh
and smile as much as any other young lady of twenty.

Unfortunately, Mr. Perrywhistle gave her very little to laugh at. At the moment he was repeating back to
her the history of her own life, pausing every so often to
verify one or two details. When she heard the sound of
Lord Frederick and Miss Perrywhistle's conversation behind her, which sounded infinitely more interesting, she
wished that she might have a different escort and racked
her brain to think of a way to accomplish it. When the
group had to stand to the side to allow some villagers to
pass them on the narrow path, she felt that perhaps this

could result in an exchange of partners. So when she did find herself at Lord Frederick's side, she was so pleased at her changed circumstance she didn't even question how it had happened.

Mr. Perrywhistle, who had tripped on Lord Frederick's strategically placed foot, knew exactly how it had happened, and resolved he wouldn't fall for such a trick again. His sister, too, had not missed Lord Frederick's eagerness to exchange partners, and she spent the rest of the walk silently fuming at her brother's side. She would have exchanged James's escort for Anthony's, but as he was escorting Lydia and Cherry, she did not see how she could accomplish it.

Lord Frederick, not at all affected by the murderous glares cast at his back, was only conscious of the timid hand that barely rested on his arm, and the joyful smile that his companion had given him; almost as if she were as pleased as he that they were finally to spend some time together.

"So, Miss Wentworth, have you been enjoying the house party?"

"Oh, yes," she said enthusiastically. "It is much better than I'd expected."

"If I remember correctly, I don't think you expected much."

"You are right," she told him. "It is a good thing my mother did not name me Hope, as I find I'm not the most hopeful of persons."

"So does *Faith* live up to her name?" he asked, and she looked up at him, a little shocked, as he said it. It was rather forward of him to use her Christian name when they were not betrothed and she had not given him permission to use it, but she knew the way he'd said it, not using it as a form of address, was perfectly proper. The way he looked at her when he said it, however, was not proper at all. And the way he hesitated as he pronounced it, as if he knew it was an intimacy she had not allowed, made it seem far too intimate, indeed.

"Yes, of course," she said, a little concerned that the conversation had taken such a personal turn so quickly. She found it was always like this with Lord Frederick. Never had she discussed with him the weather, or the state of the roads, but they must immediately begin conversations that left her stomach knotted and her heart in her throat. But, she reminded herself, she was being too serious again. So she smiled at him, saying, "That is, it depends upon which meaning of the word you refer to. I am faithful in the sense of being loyal, but I must admit to falling short of my name when it comes to having confidence in others."

"Maybe you just need to become further acquainted with people. It is difficult to have faith in someone you do not know well."

Faith felt it was not presumptuous to think he was speaking to her of himself. She still found his boldness a trifle alarming, but in keeping with her resolve not to be so serious, she merely said, "I do not have very easy manners, I'm afraid."

"You are shy," Lord Frederick said, and it sounded, on his lips, like a compliment.

"Yes, I am a little shy. I do not think you've ever been accused of that, have you, Lord Frederick?" she asked him, determined to turn the discussion away from her traits.

"No, I can't say that I have. If anything, I might be rather too straightforward. Do you find me so, Miss Wentworth?"

She was delighted at the question. It was as if he knew he had alarmed her by his boldness and was asking how she wanted things to proceed. She hoped she was not reading too much into his question, but when she looked at him, it did not seem as if she had mistook his meaning. "Yes, Lord Frederick, I must admit I am unused to such ... straightforward conversation. Perhaps you will think me hopelessly naive, but I've had little experience with..." She didn't know how to end the sentence, and wished she hadn't begun it. She looked at him for help.

"I, too, have little experience. I think we both could use more practice," he told her, with a mischievous smile.

Faith couldn't help grinning back at him, though she said, "I have no idea what it is we're actually discussing."

"I am the heartless rogue you accused me of being in town, to tease you so shamelessly. I think, what we are discussing, is friendship. I would like to get to know you better, Miss Wentworth, but I promise not to be so...straightforward about it. There's no rush, after all. Perhaps time is needed to build faith."

"I think you are right, Lord Frederick. Fortunately, I have plenty of time at present," Faith told him, giving him a playful glance. *Lady Burke would be proud of me,* she thought, not realizing the effect of that glance on Lord Frederick.

Lord Frederick began to think he erred in saying

there was no rush. Because, suddenly, capturing this woman's heart was becoming incredibly urgent. When he thought of how he would then have the freedom, not only to use her first name, but to kiss that adorable mouth and see her dusky locks loosed from their restraints, he could only think time was a horrible enemy, and wished he could have chosen to court a lady as impetuous as he. Instead, he had just promised to take things slowly.

He realized, however, that he had no other choice. Faith was like some woodland creature who, if approached too quickly, would dart away from him. She seemed, in fact, to distrust not only him but his whole sex, and he cursed her father, and perhaps her brothers, for giving her a bad impression of them all. He resolved to change that impression, though it must be admitted his was no magnanimous concern for the fraternity of man, but rather an entirely selfish motive to make her like him as much as he did her.

Nine

❧❦

The walk to the vicarage seemed much too short to Lord Frederick but the same could not be said of Miss Perrywhistle, who heaved a great sigh of relief when Sir Anthony shouted to the group that the rectory was in sight. It was a pleasant house with a well-kept garden, and the young lady who could be seen tending it appeared as attractive as Sir Anthony had said, though the color of her hair was still a bit of a mystery as it was mostly hidden by her bonnet.

However, as the group came nearer to the house Miss Foster stood up and turned to greet them, and Mr. Perrywhistle said rather loudly, "Brown hair," which caused his sister to look at him like he was crazy and Lord Frederick to try to suppress a grin.

Thankfully, Miss Foster did not hear Mr. Perrywhistle's remark, and was able to greet the large party that had descended upon her brother's house composedly enough, inviting them all to come inside. Before they could agree Sir Anthony put forth an objection to the plan. "Thank you, Miss Foster, but the young ladies are planning to visit the shops in the village. It is just Mr. Perrywhistle and myself who are here to see your brother." He then proceeded to introduce her to the rest of the party, as he was the only one with whom she was acquainted.

"Would you care to join us, Miss Foster?" Faith asked, as she had taken an instant liking to this girl with her chestnut-colored curls and sweet smile.

Miss Foster directed that smile at Faith, saying, "I thank you, Miss Wentworth, for the kind invitation, but I do not like to keep you all waiting and it would take me too long to change."

"Then you and your brother must come this evening for dinner at Kenilworth, Miss Foster, if you are to deprive the ladies of your company this morning," Sir Anthony said.

"Thank you, Sir Anthony. I would very much like to come, if my brother says we might," Miss Foster told him. Everyone smiled at the prospect of seeing the charming Miss Foster again that evening, except Miss Perrywhistle, who thought bitterly to herself there were almost as many marriageable young females in the vicinity of Kenilworth as there were at Almack's.

Before they could take their leave Mr. Foster came around from the back of the house, and Sir Anthony made more introductions.

Mr. Foster and his sister resembled each other in appearance, but Mr. Foster was seen to be a trifle more reserved than his sister, and his smile, while polite, was not as broad. He was handsome, but smaller in stature than Lord Frederick and Sir Anthony, and he wore spectacles. He looked, in fact, like a scholar, and not at all like a sportsman. Faith eyed him curiously, as he was not a type of gentleman with whom she was familiar. When he was invited to Kenilworth for dinner, the first sentence out of his mouth after his acceptance was: "I am pleased you are inviting me, because I believe you said I could make use of your library, and you have a copy of a Newton manuscript I would like to examine more carefully. It seems that Sir Isaac did not accept the divinity of Christ, and asserts the Trinity was introduced as a tenet of Christianity long after Christ's death."

Since none of the company except Faith found this remark at all interesting, and no one knew how to react to the introduction of a heavy subject like Church doctrine and possible heresy into a mindless morning stroll, there was an awkward silence following Mr. Foster's speech. However, Miss Perrywhistle could never stand to be ignored for long, so she broke it to say, "We all believed you to be a clergyman, Mr. Foster. There was no need for you to prove it."

Mr. Perrywhistle laughed at his sister's joke, but Miss Foster appeared distressed, looking quickly at her brother as if to gauge his feelings. Faith, who knew how it felt to be concerned for a family member's lack of social graces, found that she was not shy at all when it came to the unfortunate Mr. Foster. She told him, "I would be most interested in reading the manuscript myself, once you have finished with it. I have never found the Trinity to have been explicitly explained in scripture and wondered at its origin."

Miss Perrywhistle's grin faded as Mr. Foster gave Faith a smile that almost matched his sister's in sweetness. "I will let you know when I am finished reading it. I would like to hear your opinion of Newton's assertions."

Miss Perrywhistle couldn't believe it; much as she disdained the attentions of an impecunious country vicar, it appeared Faith Wentworth had made yet another conquest. And as Mr. Foster turned from smiling at Faith to look Miss Perrywhistle over, his smile gone and an enigmatic look in his eye, Diana felt it hard, indeed, that she didn't even rate a smile from him.

❧

Lord Frederick, too, was disturbed by the introduction of the good vicar into their circle. Most men would not have considered the small-statured, bespectacled Mr. Foster a serious rival, but Lord Frederick had begun to have an almost instinctual knowledge into Faith's way of thinking, and he realized that the gentleman's unthreatening nature was precisely what made him such a serious threat. Lord Frederick wondered if he should give up sport or take to wearing spectacles so that Faith would jump to his defense in such a manner. As they left the vicarage and made their way into town, Miss Perrywhistle uncharacteristically making no attempt to claim his arm and instead walking ahead of them in a fit of abstraction, Lord Frederick offered his arm to Faith again.

She accepted it happily, but immediately destroyed his hopes by saying, "Aren't you pleased the Fosters will be dining with us tonight? I think they will be a nice addition to our little party."

"I had no idea your interest inclined toward the religious. I can see I need to brush up on my theology."

"It's about the only subject I can speak of with any authority. You see, my nanny was from a family of Quakers, and she insisted I read the Bible every day. Since my other choice of reading material was a sports journal, I was not averse to the idea. She used to quiz me on what I read, and since I found her conversation more interesting than my family's, I became accustomed to theological discussions. Perhaps that is why I already feel in sympathy with the Fosters."

Wonderful, thought Lord Frederick. *She's confused Mr. Foster with a beloved childhood mentor. Perhaps she even feels it is part of the Divine Will, her meeting him.*

However, he did not let it discourage him too much. Lord Frederick may have introduced the courting game as a ploy to distract the Captain, but he truly did feel it a good idea to get to know a prospective bride before taking the irrevocable step of marriage, and he felt these past few days spent in Faith's company he'd learned a lot about her, and all of it in her favor. He now knew they were very well-suited, and he was confident she would soon begin to see that as clearly as he did.

And, though he was admittedly not as well-versed in theology as she was, he was curious to hear her opinion on that subject, also. On the walk back from the village they discussed the sad state of the current Church, in which young men who were not at all qualified to teach were ordained merely by answering a question or two, many times unrelated to religion.

"Why, our Vicar told us that at his ordination the only two questions he answered were who his mother was, and if any other gentlemen in his family were clergymen," Faith told him.

Lord Frederick had never given much thought to Church reform, though he agreed the current state of affairs were deplorable, and very unlike what the early Church fathers would have wanted. However, when Faith mentioned that Mr. Foster, at least, seemed to be a serious theologian, he quickly turned the subject. He would not waste their precious time together discussing a gentleman who could turn out to be his rival.

❧

Sir Anthony was almost as unhappy with Mr. Foster as Lord Frederick was, but for an entirely different reason. He had forgotten when he volunteered Mr. Foster for the role of referee in their game that Mr. Foster was not, by any stretch of the imagination, a gamester. He was highly unlikely to agree to help Sir Anthony with such a frivolous endeavor. Obviously some subterfuge was called for. Sweating a little under that bespectacled gaze, which called up memories of being sent up to the headmaster for some misdeed when he was a boy, he frantically tried to think.

"What can I do for you, Sir Anthony?" Mr. Foster prompted, when the silence became over-long.

Sir Anthony and Mr. Perrywhistle were sitting with Mr. Foster in the drawing room of the rectory, Miss Foster having left the gentlemen to their conversation after they had declined her offer of refreshments.

"I would appreciate your help in a matter of great delicacy," Sir Anthony finally ventured, but again stumbled to a halt.

"Yes?" Mr. Foster asked. Sir Anthony wondered how it was he'd ever been talked into giving Foster the living at Kenilworth. Foster did not display at all the

sycophantic demeanor that most recipients of such a
plum showed their benefactors. Before this morning Sir
Anthony would have said that he found such insincere
and unctuous displays annoying, which is one of the reasons he'd chosen Foster for the job, but he couldn't deny
that he wished Foster's manner was a *tad* more deferen-
tial.

"You remember Miss Wentworth, whom you
met this morning? Of course you do, that's a stupid
question. At any rate, her father is such a stickler, he's
decreed that no one can win her hand without proving
they have a thorough knowledge of her character and
habits."

"Ah, he's a wise man," Mr. Foster said. "Milton
felt somewhat similarly. He said that marriage is not a
mere carnal coition but a human society, and all human
society must proceed from the mind rather than the
body, or we would be no better than the beasts. Of
course, he was arguing for divorce at the time he wrote
it, but I think the principle is sound, don't you gentlemen agree?"

Mr. Perrywhistle was wondering if the word
"coition" meant what he thought it did, and was shocked
that a vicar would talk so broad on a morning call. He
looked at Sir Anthony for guidance, as he didn't know
how to respond.

"Yes, of course we agree. Milton was our na-
tional genius, after all. It would be unpatriotic not to
agree with him," Sir Anthony said, pleased to see his
gambit was working.

"Of course, of course," James echoed, though he
was still confused about what he had just agreed to, and

hoped that Milton fellow wasn't advocating celibacy.

"But to get back to the point at hand," Sir Anthony said. "Captain Wentworth needs some kind of proof that the applicants for his daughter's hand know her as well as they claim to. And so he's asked them to successfully pass a series of questions before permitting them to propose. Which is where you come in," Sir Anthony told Mr. Foster. "We need a disinterested party to pose the questions and test the applicants."

"But I know nothing about Miss Wentworth. How can I know if the applicants have answered the questions correctly?"

"You'll have to decide on the questions, interview the lady so that you can know her answers, and then test the gentlemen."

"You said "gentlemen." How many are competing for Miss Wentworth's hand?"

"That still is undecided, as the gentlemen have to come to a more thorough knowledge of the lady before deciding if she should suit. However, since Captain Wentworth gave his ultimatum, we've all come to agree with him that it's a good idea to have a thorough knowledge of *any* woman before entering matrimony. So we're making an experiment of the mating ritual. Whichever lady a gentleman favors, he must pass the same test before proposing. I suppose you could say we're putting into action Milton's words that marriage should proceed from the mind."

Sir Anthony knew he had won when he invoked Milton. A gleam of interest lit the vicar's eye, though he merely said, "'Whoso findeth a wife findeth a good thing.'"

"So you'll help us?"

Mr. Foster nodded. "I find myself very interested in the outcome of your experiment."

Ten

James Perrywhistle wrestled all that afternoon with a serious dilemma. He felt like he had acquired a great deal of knowledge about Miss Wentworth and he knew the importance of not changing horses mid-stream, but he also felt his sister was aware and suspicious of his attentions, and Miss Wentworth herself did not appear gladdened by his notice in the least. If anything, she seemed to view him as lacking in sense, and to be always in the company of a young lady who thought you a fool was beginning to depress him. Now there was a new young lady on the scene, Miss Foster, who seemed very agreeable and had not been singled out by any gentleman thus far. Perhaps he could begin again, and try for a little more subtlety on his second attempt.

James was perhaps the only gentleman who was actively playing the game, as Sir Anthony had no intention at all of marrying Miss Wentworth, and Lord Frederick had every intention of doing so, but viewed the game as a mere ruse to deflect the Captain from forcing a proposal from Sir Anthony until he had a chance to decide if he wanted to make one. However, he was beginning to think he'd made a tactical error in agreeing to the introduction of Mr. Foster to the game, as his role as referee would require that he spend a great deal of time with Faith, and Lord Frederick didn't want to have saved

her from Sir Anthony only to find her married to Mr.
Foster. He found himself further alarmed when, on returning to the house before dinner, he found that Mr.
and Miss Foster had walked over quite a bit earlier in
order for Mr. Foster to peruse the library, and that Faith
had spent the hours before dinner in their company.

Faith had been delighted to further her acquaintance with Miss Foster, whom she liked more and more
the more she knew of her. This young lady had none of
Miss Perrywhistle's haughty airs, but a warm-hearted nature that attracted Faith like a moth to flame. Faith,
who had experienced very little in the way of affection
after her mother's death, was overjoyed to now have the
acquaintance of two ladies, Miss Foster and Lady Burke,
who showed her *such* kindness. She wished she could
remain always at Kenilworth, and began to wonder if
marriage to Sir Anthony was so dreadful a prospect, after
all.

Of course, Miss Foster was only visiting her
brother and would not remain in the vicinity, so things
could not remain as they were. And Faith also recognized that it was quite foolish to marry a gentleman because you were infatuated with his mother! But the
thought of going home again to Eaton Park seemed almost unbearable to her. In her mind, it was as torturous
a prospect as consigning a person again to a dark cell after they had been allowed out into the light.

She had also given up the idea of Lady Burke
making a match with her father. As much as Faith might
wish for such a thing there was no reason for Lady Burke
to do so. Her father could not elevate her in situation or
social standing, and he had not the attractions, other

than his manly appearance, to tempt a lady such as Lady
Burke into matrimony.

So Faith resolved to enjoy her remaining weeks at
Kenilworth as much as she possibly could and not to
dwell too much upon her future. There was always the
prospect of letters and future visits, which would enliven
some of the dullness at Eaton Park. Cherry had improved a little as well, so even though she and Faith
would never be truly in sympathy with one another, they
could perhaps be better friends than they ever were in
the past.

Lord Frederick was already in the drawing room
when Faith and the Fosters entered together, and Lord
Frederick thought Faith looked more at ease than she'd
ever looked in their acquaintance. He hoped against
hope that it was the introduction of Miss Foster, and not
her brother, that made the difference in Faith's manner.

Lord Frederick made a point of remaining by
Faith's side so that he could have the honor of leading
her into dinner, and as James had finally settled in his
mind that Miss Foster was a more appropriate quarry, he
was successful in his bid. He was also relieved at dinner
when most of Faith's conversation was centered upon
Miss Foster, whom she had no qualms about praising to
the sky. He felt it was generous of her to praise another
so assiduously, and thought that Miss Perrywhistle, for
instance, would probably never think to converse with an
eligible gentleman about the virtues of another female,
unless it in some manner called attention to her own.

Lord Frederick was the one who finally introduced Mr. Foster into the conversation, as he was desir-
ous of knowing what had occurred between he and

Faith. "So, were you able to continue your theological discussion with Mr. Foster?" he asked, confident that Mr. Foster was too far removed from their end of the table to hear their conversation.

After Faith looked over to assure herself of the same thing, she lowered her voice to say: "To tell you the truth, I have come to regret my hasty speech a dozen times since."

This was a promising statement, but Lord Frederick tried not to appear too pleased. "Really? Why is that?"

"He now sees me as some sort of female scholar, and is recommending I read works by Rousseau and Wollstonecraft, and other heavy, philosophical tomes I have not the least interest in."

"Wollstonecraft is not *so* heavy, merely repetitive. I found her treatise tedious reading, but she made some valid points."

"You've read *A Vindication of the Rights of Women?*"

"I do read, you know, Miss Wentworth, even if I'm not a brilliant scholar like Mr. Foster."

"I realize you read, Lord Frederick, but as you are a sportsman I assumed your interests were more narrow, like my father's. He would never read anything by Wollstonecraft, or any other lady author."

"Just because I enjoy the occasional sport, I would not categorize myself a "sportsman." I also enjoy music and art, but neither am I a musician or an artist."

His comment appeared to be something of a surprise to Faith, and she studied him through narrowed eyes for a moment. "How would you categorize yourself?" she finally asked, as if she had tried to do so and failed.

"I hope I am a gentleman, but I find I have no liking for a more specific category. Why should you try to constrain a person's character by putting a tag on him?"

"But would you not agree that some persons demonstrate, by their interests and conversation, that they belong to a certain type?"

"Certainly for the purpose of brevity we might classify some persons as belonging to a type, but even within that so-called type there is variety of personality and character. I think your experience growing up in a household of sportsmen has made you feel that all men who play sports must possess the same nature and character as your father and brothers. Could that be the case?"

"Perhaps. I know, rationally, that it's not necessarily true, that there must be some gentlemen who play sports and also write poetry, for example, but I find it very difficult to believe that such gentlemen are commonly found. It seems easier to believe that there are different types of gentlemen, the Poet, the Sportsman, the Politician, etcetera, than many who possess such diverse qualities all in one form."

"There's some truth to that, but I think when you say "sportsman" you're not merely describing a gentleman who plays sport, but the term has come, in your mind, to imply someone who has no interest in any of the things that interest you. Is that not so, Miss Wentworth?"

There was a pause as Faith contemplated his

words, before having to acknowledge the truth of them. "How do you read my character so accurately, Lord Frederick? I wish I could repay the favor, so that you could see how uncomfortable it can be." She smiled as she said it, however, so he was confident she was not really offended.

"I apologize, Miss Wentworth, I had no desire to make you uncomfortable. I just desire you to know that even though I have some interest in sports, my interests are not at all confined to that sphere. I have other, far more compelling, interests."

"May I inquire into some of your other interests?"

"Certainly. I find myself very interested in shy young ladies with large grey eyes, an interest I have only lately discovered but am resolved to pursue."

Faith wished desperately she possessed a portion of Miss Perrywhistle's wit so she could make some quick reply, but found that she was not so self-possessed as that young lady, and was greatly relieved that before the silence between her and Lord Frederick could become too prolonged Lady Burke announced it was time for the ladies to retire.

"We will have to continue this conversation later," Lord Frederick murmured to her as she rose and, with a quick look at him, left the table.

❧❧

Faith was determined that the two ladies she liked so well become better acquainted with each other. So later that evening, after the gentlemen rejoined the ladies in the drawing room and Lady Burke had finished her duties with the tea urn, Faith told Lady Burke of Miss Foster's interest in gardening, as she knew that Lady Burke was also a very keen gardener.

"Miss Foster, you must come back tomorrow morning and tour the gardens here at Kenilworth," Lady Burke said.

"I would like it above all things!" Miss Foster replied.

"And Mr. Foster, you are also more than welcome to return and join the tour."

Mr. Foster bowed his acceptance of the invitation but Sir Anthony, who had begun to feel his house party, for which he'd had such high hopes, had somehow degenerated into nothing more than drawing room games and garden parties, thought it was time he steered things back on to their proper course. "Foster, if you prefer you can come with us gentlemen. We're going to take a gun out in the woods. There are quite a lot of pheasants this year."

"I'd actually prefer the garden tour, but thank you for the invitation."

"I, too, would like to tour the gardens," Lord Frederick said. "My mother would be quite disappointed if I did not give her a full report of the layout of your gardens here at Kenilworth."

"Count me in," James said, as he knew this was the perfect opportunity to make up some time with Miss Foster.

"And perhaps, after you've toured the gardens, you'd like to help me with my needle-work or read a sermon," his sister said to him in an undertone only he could hear, not at all deceived into thinking he preferred flowers over hunting.

Miss Perrywhistle had never been so annoyed in her life. Really, all the gentlemen's behavior at this house party was beyond the pale. They might as well be ladies dressed in trousers, so inexplicable were their actions. The most odious, in her view, was Mr. Foster, as she felt he was laughing at her behind his enigmatic gaze. She had thought when he first entered the drawing room after dinner that he was coming to turn the pages of her music and listen to her play, as he had come immediately to where she sat at the pianoforte. She could not help but feel thrilled that *one* gentleman, even a paltry one like Mr. Foster, preferred her over Miss Wentworth. But upon arriving at her side he had merely moved the candelabra that she had placed on top of the pianoforte, and turned to leave.

Before he could do so she stopped playing to say, "Mr. Foster, thank you for your attention to my comfort, but I could see perfectly well before you moved the candelabra."

"Yes, I am sure you could. However, as much as you might desire to set our party ablaze with your talent, I did not think you wanted to do so in a *literal* way."

Miss Perrywhistle, her usual quick wit deserting her, found nothing to say in reply. So she merely turned her back on Mr. Foster and resumed her playing. Perhaps the candles had been a *little* close to the draperies, but she was sure they would have never caught on fire and that Mr. Foster was being irritatingly officious.

Later that evening, when she overheard her brother asking Miss Foster what her favorite book was,

as if he cared a whit about such a thing, and she heard
Mr. Foster questioning Miss Wentworth similarly, her
earlier suspicions returned. She was convinced there
must be some sort of wager afoot. Her brother was
known for enacting ridiculous behavior in the pursuit of
a wager. On one occasion he had jumped backward on
one foot for 200 feet without touching the ground with
the other, and another time he built a contraption to
keep rain from touching down on a parcel of land because he had bet it would not rain there for fifteen days.
She was convinced his present, unusual behavior also
sprang from such a source. So when she was finally able
to speak to her brother out of the ear shot of others, *she*
began asking the questions, much to his dismay.

"James, what sort of game is this? Why are you
gentlemen asking so many pointed questions, and then
trying to memorize the answers?"

"Game? Who said anything about a game? I'm
merely passing the time. Miss Wentworth and Miss
Foster are two of the most attractive females of my acquaintance, so I thought I'd learn a bit about them."

"You can't fob me off with such a story; your
behavior has been far too peculiar. I have never known
you so avid in your pursuit of anything, unless it involved some form of sport."

"Nonsense," James said, flustered as his sister's
accusations were beginning to strike too close to home.
But having been involved in many arguments with his
sisters over the years, he had learned the value of mount-
ing a counter-offensive. "I believe you're jealous, because
none of the gentlemen are asking you any questions."

"Jealous?" she echoed, managing a somewhat

convincing laugh. "There has never been a more worth-less set of men anywhere I've been in residence. I begin to wish we'd not accepted our cousin's invitation."

"You can't play off your airs and graces with me, Di. You're upset because you are not coming in for your usual share of attention."

James congratulated himself on the success of his maneuver when his sister's response was to turn her back on him and stalk off in a grand manner, her attack on him forgotten for the nonce.

Eleven

❧❧

Faith was pleased when she awoke the next morning to a beautiful summer day with a blue, cloudless sky, perfect weather for a tour of the gardens. She herself had limited experience with gardening, the gardens at Eaton Park not being considered by her father as worthy as an investment as the stables, but she began to wonder if gardening might not be a new outlet for her upon her return home. No companion was necessary to garden, and she already felt there was a kind of fulfillment for the spirit in the contemplation of nature.

She thought again about the possibility that she may *not* have to return home, but this time she considered that there might be an option open to her other than marrying Sir Anthony. Perhaps another gentleman might find an interest in—what was it Lord Frederick had said? "Shy young ladies with large grey eyes." She smiled to herself as she thought of his words. She had been pleased to hear Lord Frederick had an interest in something other than sport, and even more pleased to hear he had an interest in *her*. Perhaps she was lacking in virtue and should have preferred him to express an interest in something more high-minded, but she could find no fault at all in his reply. Never had Lord Frederick made her feel that she was not so important as her father, nor made her discuss only his concerns with no reference to her own.

Up until the time of her London debut she had always believed that she would one day leave her father's house to set up housekeeping in her husband's. It was not until she was faced with the prospect of a match with Sir Anthony that she recognized being wed to someone like her father, someone with whom she shared no common interests, was a worse fate than merely being the daughter of such a man. In the past she had viewed marriage in the nature of an escape, but she now realized the wrong marriage could cause her to feel even more trapped than she did at present.

She had found herself trying so desperately to avoid marriage with Sir Anthony, marriage itself had become something to shun as well. Was it only possible in poetry to find "the marriage of true minds?" In her experience, limited as it was, gentlemen saw ladies as only an appurtenance, not a true partner in life. But perhaps life with Lord Frederick might be different. Perhaps *he* was different.

He certainly was attractive, but so was Sir Anthony. However, Sir Anthony's conversation had never sparked the nervous fluttering she experienced when Lord Frederick spoke with her. Of course, Sir Anthony never really *conversed* with her, so perhaps that is why she found Lord Frederick so superior to him. And the way he looked at her, too, with interest and admiration, would be quite exhilarating if she could just overcome her silly fears and enjoy his company. She wished she could respond in a way that would encourage Lord Frederick, as she realized her behavior to him thus far might be perceived as discouraging his attentions.

That morning, as she prepared for her walk in the gardens, she decided to give Lord Frederick an indication that his attentions were far from odious to her, though she wasn't quite sure *how* to do so.

❦

Sir Anthony, who had no desire to tour his own gardens and knew that Captain Wentworth similarly had little interest in them, was able to achieve his fondest wish: a morning spent exclusively in the illustrious Captain's company, being schooled in his theories of physical training and pedestrianism. As these involved such things as sweating treatments and partaking of emetics to induce vomiting, it could be understood why Sir Anthony did not enjoy this occasion as much as he'd fondly anticipated. However, the sacrifice was worthwhile if it resulted in "increased musculature and athletic performance," which Sir Anthony was assured by Captain Wentworth would be the case, if he only promised to keep to the program a few weeks a year. Sir Anthony, while in the Captain's company, had no problem promising such a thing, but could not be faulted if he found himself little desiring to embark on such a course when his trainer was no longer there to encourage him.

Lydia and Cherry were also uninterested in the garden tour and had told Lady Burke they preferred to ride, but if that ride took them to the back of the stable yard behind a hedge, where they could dismount and look through a gap and observe Sir Anthony lifting dumb bells and throwing logs at the Captain's command, only they knew of it. In actuality it was a boring performance, not worth the effort they'd put forth to see it, but knowing that they were not supposed to be viewing it and that they were successful in doing so made it all very thrilling.

The rest of the party, other than Mrs. Perrywhistle, who sat in splendid isolation in the drawing room with her tambour frame, duly presented themselves after breakfast for their garden tour. Lady Burke led the tour and Miss Perrywhistle, Mr. Perrywhistle, the Fosters, Faith and Lord Frederick followed with every appearance of pleasure.

Miss Perrywhistle's pleasure quickly diminished when Lord Frederick and Faith paired up, as well as James and Miss Foster, which left her at the annoying Mr. Foster's side. She was quite familiar with the gardens at Kenilworth, having visited her cousin's family on several occasions before, and was unsure why she was wearing her most becoming morning dress (which was certain to be ruined by grass stains) for what was likely to be a very dull morning spent at the side of a man far beneath her notice.

Faith, however, was enthralled with the tour. Lady Burke had begun by showing them the "Red Book" that Humphry Repton, the renowned landscape gardener, had made before work began on the gardens, and so they were able to see an illustration of how it had all looked fifteen years ago before his designs were implemented. She had never seen anyone attempt a manipulation and enhancement of nature on such a grand scale, and she was impressed and awed by the talent displayed.

There was an upper and lower terrace that led down to the park, and an avenue of trees that led into a woodland garden. All had been designed to create vistas in every direction, and Faith wished she were skilled at painting so she might capture one of the many out-standing views.

Lord Frederick also enjoyed the tour, and thought he might incorporate some of the ideas at Don-well, his own, smaller estate. But he found the expres-sion of wonder and delight on Faith's face just as appeal-ing as the beauty of the gardens, and so divided his time between looking at the two.

Faith caught him staring at her, but remembering her resolve she did not blush and look away from the admiration she saw in his eyes. She couldn't entirely overcome her shyness so was not able to meet and hold his gaze for very long, but it was long enough for her to see he had interpreted her smile correctly, and returned it.

She looked back at the rhododendrons and azal-eas that were blooming profusely, but the colors seemed to blur before her eyes, and she missed some of Lady Burke's comments identifying a few of the lesser known tree specimens. Lord Frederick's slow, teasing smile was powerful enough to blind her temporarily to the other beauty around her.

Poor Miss Foster, on whose behalf the garden tour had been arranged, was missing a large portion of Lady Burke's commentary as her escort, Mr. Perrywhis-tle, seemed determined to talk to her through the entire tour. Finally, after he had asked her twice which ladies' seminary she had attended, she lost total patience with him.

"Mr. Perrywhistle, please! I am trying to attend

to Lady Burke."

As even an impatient Miss Foster could not be truly unkind, her tone with him was not as fierce as she'd thought. Mr. Perrywhistle, however, had been directing all of his questions to the top of her bonnet and this was the first time Miss Foster had looked directly at him, her face flushed in her agitation and her eyes meeting his. He found, to his great surprise, that the sight affected him in some strange manner. All of a sudden, the only question he could think to ask was whether or not she had left any beaux behind in Kent, but this seemed such a forward question he obediently became silent, walking by the lady's side as if in a daze.

The vivacious Diana Perrywhistle had also been unusually quiet. She was not normally inclined to find her pleasures in nature, but the weather was so comfortable, the scenery so beautiful, and her companions so awed, that she could not help but begin to feel a similar sense of wonder. When they exited a woodland path and found they were at the top of a small hill with a lake surrounded by deer spread out enticingly below them she heard Mr. Foster murmur: "O Lord, how manifold are thy works! in wisdom hast thou made them all: the earth is full of thy riches" and she had no desire at all to ridicule him for the sentiment. In fact, she felt like replying "Amen," and wondered that people congregated in musty churches when a walk through the woods had such a spiritually uplifting effect.

But when they eventually came to the bottom of a set of steps that led up to a gazebo the spell was broken, and James Perrywhistle could not help himself; he challenged Lord Frederick to a race to the top.

"It is two hundred steps," Lady Burke warned, "but the view is quite unparalleled; you can actually see the ocean. However, I have no intention of climbing so many steps, and will return to the house. There is a cold collation in the dining room, and when you are through with your explorations you are all welcome to join me there."

Lord Frederick was tempted to race James, he was sure he could beat him, but was also hopeful that he could perhaps lead Faith down a garden path, in a literal way only, of course. He was also afraid if he left her side Mr. Foster would take his place, as he had seen him eyeing them a few times. He looked down at his companion, who was wearing a worried expression.

"Are you sure it's safe to race?" she asked him. "The steps are quite narrow."

Lord Frederick had no fears for his safety but was pleased Faith did. "I think it is safe, but I'd rather stay by your side. Would you like to go up? If not, we could go back to see the folly. We did no more than take a quick glance at it."

Faith looked around to see what the others intended to do. Miss Foster had decided to walk part of the way back to the house with Lady Burke to ask her about the portions of the tour she had missed, and James, seeing Miss Foster walking away, took a few steps after her but then turned back toward the gazebo.

"Well? Is anyone coming?" James Perrywhistle asked, before beginning his ascent.

Lord Frederick turned to Miss Perrywhistle. "Miss Perrywhistle? Will you go up?"

Diana, delighted by his attention, said, "If you

mean to give me your arm, I believe I will."

With a well-simulated look of disappointment Lord Frederick told her: "Unfortunately, Miss Wentworth is a little fatigued and I promised to escort her somewhere she can sit and rest before tackling the steps. Mr. Foster, will you give Miss Perrywhistle your arm?"

"Certainly," Mr. Foster said, his manner giving nothing away, but Lord Frederick was sure he had scored a victory over him and was vastly pleased with himself for maneuvering things so well. Diana, with a scornful glance at Faith, took Mr. Foster's arm and began to climb the steps.

Faith said nothing until the other couple was out of ear shot; then, turning to Lord Frederick, said, "I really am not at all fatigued and would have liked to see the view. Now Miss Perrywhistle thinks me a feeble creature."

"Surely you do not care what she thinks of you."

"I would like to pretend I do not, but she quite intimidates me."

"She is merely jealous."

"I cannot think why she should be," Faith replied, truly mystified.

"I can think of a dozen reasons, but let us not spoil our time together talking of *her*."

Faith was more than pleased to put Diana Perrywhistle and her sneering glance from her mind, and followed her escort down the path that led to the Grecian temple folly. However, she was a bit apprehensive. She wondered if she should have gotten advice from Lady Burke on what was the appropriate amount of encouragement to give a gentleman. She didn't think Lord

Frederick a rake but, then again, he'd never said a word about having any honorable attentions toward her. He'd obviously planned to separate her from the rest of the party, and Mrs. Tibbet had frequently told her she should never be alone with a gentleman unless they were betrothed. The silence seemed to grow heavy between them; Faith too shy to meet Lord Frederick's gaze and unable to think of a thing to say to dispel the atmosphere that seemed to have overtaken them.

It was, however, the middle of the day and they were just a few minutes from the house. Surely her fears were groundless. She looked up at Lord Frederick and surprised a look in his eye that did not assuage her fears in the least. Not minding her step, she tripped on the gravel path and Lord Frederick caught her in his arms.

∂∞∂

By the time Diana and Mr. Foster made it to the gazebo, Diana's mood had improved tremendously. She was rather proud of herself for her accomplishment in climbing two hundred steps and though somewhat breathless, she was in an exultant mood. Out of all the young ladies, *she* was the only one brave enough to climb to the top, and she exchanged a victorious look with her escort. He actually smiled at her, and Diana was astounded at the effect it had on her. She really must be out of breath if a mere smile from a man she detested could make her feel so strange.

Diana was a little surprised that Mr. Foster, in spite of the fact he was not a large man, was still quite strong. She'd made good use of his arm on the way up and it was not the arm of a weakling. Even after their brisk climb he was not winded like she was.

"'Pon my word, it's quite a view, what?" James said to his sister and Mr. Foster when they arrived at the top, and Diana could almost wish James was not there. She'd come to appreciate the fact that Mr. Foster did not mouth polite inanities. It was much more peaceful than James's constant nattering on about nothing.

But Diana did agree that the view was spectacular. They could see for miles around, and could even just make out the ocean, as Lady Burke had promised. Looking toward the house they saw Miss Foster had left Lady Burke and was walking back in their direction.

James had already spent some time admiring the view while he waited for his sister and Mr. Foster to arrive, and he was now ready to make his descent. Particularly as he hoped to meet Miss Foster on the path.

"I say, are you two ready to go back down?"

"No, you go ahead, I need to catch my breath. We'll be down in a few minutes," Diana told him, without even waiting for Mr. Foster's agreement. But when she looked at him after James left, she could not make out his expression at all. She felt a little nervous at her presumptuousness, and could not understand why this man disturbed her peace so much. She walked over to look out the other side of the gazebo, and saw Faith Wentworth and Lord Frederick walking on the gravel path that led to the Grecian folly.

"She must not have been *too* fatigued," Diana said, nodding in the direction of the couple.

Mr. Foster didn't reply, but continued to stare at Miss Wentworth and Lord Frederick. This infuriated

Diana, who was irritated she could not even retain the interest of the gentleman by her side. "What is so wondrous exciting about the girl?" she asked him.

"Are you referring to Miss Wentworth?"

"No, I'm talking about Sally, my maid. Of course I'm referring to Miss Wentworth. What do you gentlemen find so attractive about her?"

"She does possess a certain dignity, mixed with an air of fragility, that is quite captivating," Mr. Foster said.

This was not the correct response, in Diana's view. Her delight in her climb quite spoiled, she stared broodingly down at the couple walking in the garden path, and saw Miss Wentworth fall into Lord Frederick's arms.

"It's a trick!" she said immediately, disappointed she did not think of trying something similar when she walked with Lord Frederick yesterday.

"It is time for us to go down," Mr. Foster told her, pulling her with him to the steps opposite, so she could no longer see the embracing couple.

৵৽৾

When Faith ended up in Lord Frederick's arms she almost screamed, so nervous had she made herself. However, Lord Frederick's expression was so far from that of a ravenous satyr she immediately felt like a fool for her suspicions of him. His concern was entirely for her welfare, and he asked anxiously if she'd hurt herself. She quickly assured him that she was fine and his brow cleared in relief. He smiled at her, still holding her in his arms.

"I am sorry to have upset you; I am not usually so clumsy," she said, as his expression grew more serious and his arms tightened around her.

"Faith, you have no idea what you do to me," he said, kissing her cheek, her brow.

Her fear of him had vanished, and she looked up at him in wonder, thinking that *this* feeling, of being safe, protected, and cherished, was one she'd never experienced in her life before now. He had drawn away from her, promising himself that those chaste kisses were all he'd take, that he wouldn't kiss her lips until they were betrothed, but he was lost when he looked in her eyes.

"Just one kiss, Faith, please? You won't run away into the woods, will you?" he asked, but Faith had no intention of going anywhere, and though she did not answer his question with words he was sure she inclined her face closer to his, which he took as an affirmative reply.

He bent the short distance and captured her mouth with his own, that sweet mouth that haunted his dreams. He drew back sooner than he wanted, still worried lest he frighten her, but she did not appear frightened. She opened her eyes and smiled at him, and he said, "Just one more, I promise" and kissed her again.

This time he did frighten her, as she was not sure how many kisses were acceptable but he had said he'd only kiss her twice, and he kissed her far more times than that, though he barely gave her time to draw breaths between kisses and she could not keep count herself.

"Lord Frederick," she finally said, turning her

face away from his, "you said just twice."

"I must have been mad," he said, pulling her head against his chest. He did not try to kiss her again but merely held her in his arms, where she could feel his heart beating as wildly as her own.

"I have never felt this way before," he said. "You are so lovely, so very lovely," he told her, and she was tempted to let him kiss her again, but knew she had to find the strength to pull away.

"We—perhaps we should join the others," she said, pulling away from his embrace and wondering how she could behave as if nothing had happened, when her whole world had changed.

"Tell me first, tell me you feel the same. No one will kiss you ever again, just me," Lord Frederick said, grabbing both her hands in his.

"Only you," Faith agreed, though she did not know what she was agreeing to. Was this a marriage proposal?

Lord Frederick was hardly in a better state. He wanted to propose but felt he should talk to her father first, and he was overcome by the strength of his feelings. He hadn't intended to kiss her, only to woo her, and he wasn't even sure she would accept him should he offer. Should he apologize? Confess his love?

Before he could do either, they heard the crunching of footsteps on the gravel path, and realized their privacy was almost at an end. Faith's eyes flew to his, this time a horrified expression in them.

"No one will know," he said, though he was not ready to face anyone himself. He straightened Faith's bonnet and gave her his arm, just before Mr. Foster and

Diana Perrywhistle came around a bend in the path.

Lord Frederick assured himself again that no one could possibly know what had just occurred, though Diana Perrywhistle looked as if she knew exactly what had been going on. He could feel Faith's hand trembling where she had laid it on his arm and he patted it briefly, and Diana's eagle eye did not miss that gesture, either.

"How are you feeling, Miss Wentworth? Did you have a chance to rest?" she asked Faith.

Lord Frederick answered on her behalf. "Actually she fell on the path, and so I am escorting her back to the house."

"Oh, no! You must be more careful, Miss Wentworth. Lord Frederick, you should have caught her."

There was an awkward silence, and Lord Frederick wondered if the blasted woman possessed occult powers. Mr. Foster murmured something Lord Frederick could not catch, but Diana heard it and turned red.

"I could do with a rest myself," she said, and stalked off without waiting for the others.

Lord Frederick was grateful to Mr. Foster for vanquishing the enemy but he now wished Foster would take himself off as well. However, Mr. Foster merely asked Faith how she was feeling and if she needed another arm to lean upon. She declined his offer, saying she was perfectly fine, and the three walked back to the house together.

"What did you say to Miss Perrywhistle?" Lord Frederick asked Mr. Foster.

"I had been reading Homer and a quotation came to mind. It was nothing of consequence."

Seeing that Mr. Foster would not tell him any

more Lord Frederick did not question him further, and Mr. Foster and Diana were the only two who knew he'd said to her: "'Oh! woman, when to ill thy mind is bent, all hell contains no fouler fiend.'"

Twelve

⊱⊰

The walk back to the house was a quiet one as Mr. Foster was not given to a lot of conversation, and Lord Frederick and Faith were both caught up in their own tumultuous thoughts and feelings. Faith's feelings alternated between giddy excitement and grave misgivings. She felt that Lord Frederick would not have taken such liberties with her if he had no intention of marrying her, but she wondered that he had not said as much before they were interrupted. However, she reassured herself that he had not much time to say anything, and that prior to the appearance of Mr. Foster and Miss Perrywhistle he had been much too preoccupied to speak. This thought, improper as it was, made her smile, and she peeped up at Lord Frederick hoping to read his countenance. He was frowning a little when she glanced up at him, but when he saw her smile his expression changed, and the warmth in his eyes made her look down again before Mr. Foster could wonder why she was blushing so.

When they reached the house the gentlemen went directly into the dining room but Faith excused herself, saying she would join them shortly. She ran up to her room, feeling she had to have some time alone to try to comprehend these strange new feelings before facing the rest of the house party.

She really wished she had someone in whom she could confide. Her governess had taught her the etiquette of polite society but Faith understood nothing of romantic relationships between the sexes other than what she'd gleaned from books. She'd known instinctively that Mrs. Tibbet was not the appropriate person to guide her, but while she trusted Lady Burke she felt she could not discuss *kissing* with her, it would be far too embarrassing. Perhaps if she and Miss Foster became better acquainted she could discuss her concerns with her.

She went down to the dining room resolved to further her friendship with Jane Foster, but she found that Diana Perrywhistle, of all people, suddenly desired her companionship. Diana greeted Faith as soon as she entered the room and requested her to sit down next to her at the table, and Faith had no choice but to agree.

Diana could be absolutely charming when she exerted herself, and Faith soon felt that she had misjudged the young lady, as she was not at all as haughty and unpleasant as she'd previously thought. After luncheon ended Diana asked if Faith would like to accompany her to her room, as she had purchased some ribbons in the village that had turned out to be entirely the wrong color for her, but that she felt would suit Faith very well. As the Fosters were leaving then to return to the vicarage Faith felt she may as well go upstairs with Diana, even though she thought Lord Frederick looked a little disappointed when she left.

After they reached Diana's room and Faith had gratefully accepted the ribbons, Diana stopped her before she could leave.

"Please stay a moment. I am happy to have this time to speak in private with you, because there is something I must tell you, Faith."

"Certainly, Diana, what is it?"

"It's a little embarrassing, actually, as it involves my brother. I'm not sure if you've ever experienced the humiliation when someone connected to you doesn't behave as they ought."

Faith knew that feeling perhaps better than anyone else, but she merely nodded her sympathy.

"Then you'll understand when I tell you that my brother is a gamester, and he frequently indulges in ridiculous behavior in pursuit of a wager, but this time I feel he's gone too far."

"I know how you feel, Diana. My father and brothers are inclined to behave similarly. But what is it that has so upset you?"

"I've discovered that the game…" Diana paused, looking sadly at Faith before continuing, "involves you."

"Involves me? How can that be?"

"I am not sure exactly, my brother would not tell me everything, but I believe that the gentlemen have wagered to see who can gain your favor the fastest. Haven't you noticed that my brother, and some of the other gentlemen, have shown you a great deal of attention?" She didn't wait for Faith to respond, but hurriedly continued: "Perhaps it is as innocent as discovering your tastes and interests, but I am concerned that it also involves a less innocent goal, like winning some demonstration of your favors, such as a kiss or *embrace*." Diana said this as if it were the most heinous activity in which Faith could involve herself, and Faith was instantly reminded of what had occurred between her and Lord Frederick that very morning, and resolved that Diana would never know of it.

But then she thought about what Diana had just said. She said the *gentlemen* had wagered on her favors. Could that be why Lord Frederick had kissed her? Could she be nothing more than a *game* to him? She, who despised such frivolous and irresponsible behavior, was now the subject of a wager? It was very upsetting, if true. And she remembered what Lord Frederick had said to her just a few hours ago: "No one will kiss you again, just me." How foolish of her to think such a thing amounted to a proposal! He was probably just ensuring she would not allow another gentlemen to win the game. Not that she would, of course; kissing Lord Frederick had been punishment enough.

For if he had no serious interest in her and meant merely to toy with her feelings, she felt it had been a very regrettable interlude, one that was already causing her painful remorse. When she remembered how cherished she felt in his arms she felt stabbed to the heart that it had all been a facade. Was there no one who could truly care for her? Was she always to have her foolish hopes dashed to pieces?

Diana, who was waiting for her to reach the conclusion she just reached, saw her sorrowful expression and felt a twinge of guilt. If Faith and Lord Frederick were truly in love with each other what she had done was not at all admirable. It was truly "foul" and "fiendish." She hoped that Mr. Foster would never discover it.

❧❧

Cherry's morning, too, had ended with an unpleasant revelation. While she and Lydia were observing Sir Anthony's training they overheard something very peculiar. Most of the conversation between he and the Captain until that point had consisted of grunts and counting, and as the thrill of having successfully accomplished their covert mission had worn off they were bored and had decided to leave. Before they could do so they heard the Captain ask Sir Anthony, "How's the game progressing? Seems like you should have won by now. Just a few questions, right? How hard can it be? And Faith's a decent girl; none of those confounded airs and graces with her. Ask her a question and she'll give you an honest answer."

Sir Anthony's reply was indistinguishable to the eavesdroppers, but they had no problem at all hearing the Captain, who always spoke in a loud tone.

"I probably shouldn't have agreed to the delay, but we're stuck here for a few weeks anyway, so I thought there was no harm in it. I must admit, though, I'd much rather see *you* win Faith's hand. The other gentlemen are well enough, but a woman needs a strong hand on the reins."

As Sir Anthony responded to this speech by running to the bushes and vomiting just a few feet from where the girls were listening, the conversation was effectively over, and Cherry and Lydia were now even more eager to leave the vicinity.

After they had snuck away and were out of ear shot of the gentlemen, Lydia turned excitedly to Cherry. "So Sir Anthony intends to make a match with your sister," she said, having no idea that such a thing would be anything more than an interesting piece of gossip to the other girl.

"I don't think he does," Cherry said, still reeling from the idea that she'd have to call that particular gentleman 'Brother.' "It seemed like it was entirely my father's idea. There is something strange going on. Please don't mention it to anyone else, Lydia. I'd hate to see Sir Anthony persuaded to form a connection he does not desire."

In Cherry's mind it was poor Sir Anthony who was being coerced and manipulated, and Faith featured in her thoughts as the villainess. So she returned to the house later that afternoon determined to reproach her sister for her shameless behavior toward Sir Anthony.

After searching the house Cherry finally found Faith in her room, lying on the bed, where she had retired immediately after her conversation with Diana. Faith had thought she'd be able to cry some of the pain away, but the tears would not come and so she just lay there trying to think of some way she could disappear, because she would never find the courage to face anyone ever again, particularly Lord Frederick.

Her sister had entered the room without knocking and Faith was alarmed at first, but seeing it was only Cherry said rather feebly, "I'm sorry, Cherry, I'm not feeling well. Can you come back some other time?"

Cherry ignored her request saying, "Faith, it can't be true! Why would Sir Anthony ever want to marry *you*?"

For some reason these words had the effect of making the tears finally start, and Faith tried to hide her face in her pillow. Cherry was right: no one wanted to

marry her. Sir Anthony was merely interested in her father's career; Lord Frederick was trying to win a game.
What was so wrong with her?

Cherry was alarmed to see her sister begin to cry
and realized her words could possibly be construed as an
insult. So she bounced onto the bed, awkwardly patting
her sister's shoulder and telling her not to cry.

"I'm sorry, Faith, I didn't mean to upset you, but
I truly do not think you and Sir Anthony are well-
matched."

"I have absolutely no feelings for Sir Anthony,"
Faith managed to say, "nor he for me. Why should he?
I am unlovable," she said, between sobs.

Now Cherry was really worried. Her older sister
was admittedly more feminine in her behavior than she
herself was, but Faith was not given to crying, and now
she wept as if her heart was broken. Had Sir Anthony
done this to her sister?

"Faith, Faith, please stop crying and tell me what
is wrong. I will fix it," Cherry promised, though when
she thought of how she'd last seen Sir Anthony, lying
weak and white-faced on the ground near a hedge, she
wondered what she could do to make him feel any more
miserable then he currently did.

Faith finally managed to compose herself and, to
her great surprise, found herself confiding in her little
sister. She told Cherry of her unsuccessful season in
town, and of Sir Anthony's interest in her when he discovered who her father was, and what she had just
learned from Diana.

"I do not trust Diana Perrywhistle," Cherry said.
"I think she is jealous of you."

"That is what he, I mean Lord Frederick, told me also, but Cherry, I do believe she is right when she said there is some kind of game going on. Her brother's behavior toward me has been extremely strange, and then, this morning, Lord Frederick..." Faith had finally stopped crying but she still found it difficult to complete her sentence.

"He what?" Cherry asked, thinking perhaps she had another target for her vengeance, now that Sir Anthony had been exonerated.

"He kissed me," Faith whispered, turning red with embarrassment and avoiding her sister's gaze.

"Really? What was it like?" Cherry asked, her tone not at all condemnatory.

Faith did not know how to respond to that question. If she were now engaged to Lord Frederick she would have no hesitation saying she enjoyed the kisses very much, but now that she thought them part of a game she was ambivalent about her feelings. "If Diana had not told me about the wager I would have thought his kisses evidence of his affection for me, but now I do not know what to think."

"I think Lord Frederick does like you Faith; I had already noticed it. He always runs to your side whenever we're all in company together, and he frequently stares at you when you're in conversation with someone else."

"But that could all be because of some wretched bet."

"I don't think so; I have never noticed Sir Anthony doing likewise."

"But there is also James Perrywhistle's behavior

to consider. His first evening here he would not leave my side and asked me all kind of odd questions."

Cherry paused at this remark, trying to remember exactly what she'd overheard that morning. "Yes, Papa said something to Sir Anthony about asking you questions as well, that Sir Anthony needed to do so in order to win your hand. But perhaps he was just urging him to propose?"

"I wish I knew what was afoot. It is very disconcerting to have my feelings toyed with in this manner, and to be the target of some foolish gentlemen's wager."

Cherry, who had never felt gaming or sport at all reprehensible, had to acknowledge that this was not a very admirable situation, and entered into her sister's feelings completely. For the first time in their lives she sided with Faith against their father, and the sisters were in better harmony with each other than they'd ever been. Cherry even made Faith feel like she could face Lord Frederick again, telling Faith that, whatever the game was, she did not think it could involve kissing.

"Because you know Papa would never countenance such a thing," Cherry told Faith, and Faith was forced to see the logic of that argument. "He did say he wished Sir Anthony to win your hand, so perhaps the gentlemen are attempting to woo you, but Papa would call Lord Frederick out if he knew he'd trifled with you."

Faith, alarmed at the notion of her father challenging Lord Frederick to a duel, told Cherry she must never tell anyone he'd kissed her.

"Of course I will not! I am no gossip," Cherry told her, insulted that her sister would think she'd betray her confidence.

"But Cherry, what should I do?" Faith asked her, though if someone had told her four-and-twenty hours ago that she'd be asking advice of her ramshackle sister she would never have believed it.

"You need not *do* anything," Cherry said. But then, remembering her earlier fear, hurried to add: "Though if Sir Anthony does propose, you should refuse him."

"That goes without saying. But what about Lord Frederick?"

"I am not sure. Do you think you would like to be married to him?"

"I am not completely certain, but yes, I *think* I would," she said, remembering again how cherished she'd felt in his arms, and the expression in his eyes as he'd held her. Surely *that* could not have been feigned. "But now I wonder if I can trust my happiness to any gentleman."

"Just be patient, Faith. There's no need to rush into any engagement. Perhaps you should refuse to be alone with Lord Frederick until we find out exactly what is going on."

Faith thought this very wise advice, as she still felt herself at fault for allowing Lord Frederick to kiss her, and she was not totally convinced she would be strong enough to stop him should he try again.

Thirteen

❧❧

Sir Anthony tracked down Lord Frederick as soon as his training session was finished and dragged him into his study.

"You have to help me," Sir Anthony told him.

As Sir Anthony looked as if he were a few steps from the grave, Lord Frederick thought at first his need was physical. "Should I send for the doctor?" he asked Sir Anthony, insisting that he sit down.

"What? No! I mean, you have to propose to Miss Wentworth immediately, her father cannot be put off any longer."

Lord Frederick was distracted, however, by the smells emanating from his friend. "What is that sour smell?" he asked, sniffing. "It smells like a lady's vinaigrette."

"What? Oh, you're right, it's vinegar. I soaked my feet in it five times, to roughen them. The Captain says it makes it easier to walk long distances."

"I'd suggest that you now soak them in cologne, unless your plan is to wave your feet under some poor faint lady's nose."

Sir Anthony shook his head at his friend's attitude. "You're proving to be a bit of a disappointment, Frederick. Spending all your time with the ladies. James, too, hardly has time for sport these days and when I just ran into him on my way into the house all he could talk about was Miss Foster's eyes." Before Anthony could complain further, his stomach made a loud rumbling noise and he turned even paler.

"Anthony, you'd better go lie down. I'll see you at dinner."

"Don't mention the word," Anthony said, clasping his hand to his mouth. He staggered from his chair over to the sofa, where he collapsed.

"I must say, the Captain's training methods do not appear to be very efficacious."

Anthony merely grunted, his eyes closed. Frederick turned to leave the room. "If you're sure you don't need a doctor, I'll leave you." Anthony waved him away. "But don't worry about Miss Wentworth. I have every intention of proposing, as soon as I possibly can."

Anthony managed a sickly smile, and Frederick left him, though he went directly to find Sir Anthony's man and suggest he attend his master in the study.

ॐ

Sir Anthony was too sick to join them at dinner that night and, when they had all been seated around the dining table without him, the Captain surveyed the appetizing food that had been laid out and shook his head in dismay. "Poor Sir Anthony," he told those seated next to him. "His constitution's been ruined by too many delicate foods."

Faith shot him a look of warning, and he desisted from too many more criticisms of his hostess's table, but he himself only took a little meat and bread and frowned sadly when he saw the unhealthy choices his fellow diners were making.

Sir Anthony's absence appeared to have cast a pall over the rest of the party, as the meal was a quiet one. James stared silently into space, Faith was making a brave attempt to appear as if her heart had not been nearly broken but was not entirely successful, and Diana was becoming acquainted with a very disagreeable part of her character previously unknown to her: her conscience. Particularly when she looked at Faith, who would not meet her eyes and was obviously in very low spirits, did she wish she could turn back the clock and undo her stupid, ignoble behavior. She didn't even have the desire to gain the advantage by flirting with Lord Frederick now that she'd vanquished her rival. On the contrary, she felt that if Faith and Lord Frederick were to announce their engagement she'd be the first to raise her glass in a toast.

Lord Frederick sensed Faith's distress but, unaware of its cause, attributed it to his own conduct. No gently-bred young lady would welcome a gentleman's advances with no assurance as to his intentions. He cursed himself for his impatience but he could not completely regret his behavior that morning, as he'd always remember that moment as the one where he'd become irrevocably convinced of his love for Faith. He was determined to speak to her father when the gentlemen were left to their port, and was disappointed when the Captain made his excuses as soon as dinner was over and left the room.

Lord Frederick was further disappointed to find when he and James joined the ladies in the drawing room that Faith had already retired for the night. He also could not help but notice that Cherry was eyeing him in a suspicious manner. He thought perhaps Faith had told her what had occurred between them that morning, and wondered if Cherry intended to ask him his intentions toward her sister or even challenge him to a duel, she was glaring at him so ferociously. It was too bad he could not announce his betrothal to Faith that very evening.

❦

The next morning was Sunday and the party made its way to church, where the pleasure of hearing Mr. Foster speak awaited them. Faith was genuinely curious to hear the Vicar, as she had recognized he was not a typical representative of the Church of England, and she hoped for something a little meatier than a re-reading of Hugh Blair's sermons, which is what occurred every Sunday in her home parish.

She was more than satisfied with the experience, as Mr. Foster did not content himself with speaking in vague terms of Christian duty or drily repeating another's words. His preaching was thought-provoking and even a bit soul-stirring. Lord Frederick was surprised that the passionless Mr. Foster was so passionate a speaker, and he looked over at Faith in some dismay. If even *he* was moved by the Vicar's words he feared Faith might have her head completely turned by the surprising parson.

Diana Perrywhistle was also quite impressed with Mr. Foster. She even thought that should a lady marry an *eloquent* clergyman, it would not be such a step down as she had always felt. A man who spoke so well in public was bound to engender respect, and the wife of such a man could not be totally disregarded, either. However, she dismissed that thought in contemplating the theme of his discourse. He had spoken on a text from the book of James, where worldly wisdom and Divine wisdom were contrasted. The first was said to be earthly, sensual, and devilish, as well as envying. She could not help but feel he was speaking directly to her, knowing what her recent behavior had been. She wished she could gaze at him freely as he spoke; he seemed to her to grow in stature and beauty as he stood there, imploring her to be a better person than she knew she was. But she was forced to look down for most of his sermon, as her beleaguered conscience would not permit her to meet his steady gaze.

Poor Diana, for once in her life she had been made to feel her inferiority, and by one she hoped to impress above all others! She was now more than willing to admit that Faith deserved every attention she received; surely *she* would not have played such a trick on another young lady. Faith was the very embodiment of Divine wisdom: "pure, peaceable, gentle, without hypocrisy…" As Mr. Foster spoke those words some of Diana's spirit reasserted itself. Surely she could become just as worthy a lady as Faith? It couldn't be too late for her to change her ways; she wasn't irredeemable at twenty-two. Perhaps if she spoke to Mr. Foster, asked him how she could apply his counsel, he would be pleased with her efforts. In vain did she try to convince herself it was God she should be interested in pleasing; she found she was still more focused on an earthly reward than a heavenly one.

&∽⧸

Faith had made an appointment with Miss Foster to spend the afternoon and evening with her at the Vicarage, and unknowingly caused disappointment in the breasts of nearly half the members of her party.

Lord Frederick and Diana Perrywhistle were overcome with envy, as Diana envied Faith her proximity with Mr. Foster and Lord Frederick was jealous of the Vicar, even though both felt the irony of indulging in such a feeling after that morning's sermon. James Perrywhistle, who was suffering from a malady he could not name, but which caused him some kind of speechless agitation whenever he was in company with Miss Foster, was disappointed he would not again have the privilege of being plagued with such suffering that afternoon.

Faith herself had a wonderful time, as she was greeted most sincerely as an honored guest, her opinions sought and her preferences attended to, and she began to realize what felicity there could be in a domicile where women were not only seen but heard. The only discomfort she had was that Mr. Foster was considerably more erudite than she and she was ignorant of many of the authors he wanted to discuss. However, as his sister similarly had little interest in "such dry, tedious stuff" they went on to discuss more familiar topics, and Faith found herself for the first time in her life weighing in on current political and social issues and finding her thoughts meeting with interest and approval.

Perhaps because of her unhappy experience at

Mrs. Tibbet's hands or because of a natural modesty Faith did not view each gentleman she met as a prospective marriage mate. Lord Frederick would have been pleased to know that a match with Mr. Foster had never even entered her head. However, sitting with him in his cozy parlor with Miss Foster by her side, both of them wearing their sweet smiles, she found herself wishing that she had known Mr. Foster better before Lord Frederick had kissed her.

കbirths

    She did not see the other members of the house party until the following morning at breakfast, when she was inundated with questions about how she'd enjoyed the previous evening.

    Lady Burke merely said how pleased she was to have Faith back at *her* table, and that they'd greatly missed her at dinner, but Diana couldn't bear not knowing every detail about what had occurred, and asked Faith about the food that was served, and if the dining room was handsome, etc. etc.

    "And did Mr. Foster take his port in solitary splendor?" Diana asked, trying to sound as if she felt herself superior to a dinner at the Vicarage.

    "No, he joined us in the drawing room. I do not think he is overly given to spirits," Faith replied.

    "How abstemious of him," Lord Frederick said, a little sarcastically, as he was sick to death of Mr. Foster. "Does he also wear hair shirts and fast?"

    Frederick was surprised when Diana turned to glare at him as fiercely as Faith did. "I believe he does all that is proper, Lord Frederick," said Faith. "Not every gentleman must be a 'three-bottle man.'"

Frederick could have cursed himself for his criticism of Mr. Foster, as it must put him firmly, in Faith's mind at least, in the ranks of those wastrels who ignored the ladies in favor of getting drunk with the men every night after dinner. Before he had an opportunity to beg her pardon Lady Burke announced that she had planned an expedition for them all.

"There is a Gothic ruin, an old church, within walking distance that is extremely picturesque. I know you young people; always on the search for the picturesque, though if you intend to engage me in a debate about whether or not it is really picturesque or merely sublime I will not speak to you ever again. It is all such pretentious folly, and I don't intend to waste time I could spend actually *enjoying* a landscape in a discussion of it."

All of those at breakfast had to smile at Lady Burke's statement, and the party broke up to prepare for their expedition. Diana Perrywhistle, however, stayed behind to beg her hostess excuse her from the morning's expedition.

"But, Diana, I thought you enjoyed watercolors."

"Yes, and perhaps I'll walk over to the ruins another time. This morning, however, I find I am not in the mood to paint."

Lady Burke kindly excused her from the excursion and Diana waited until they all had departed, before walking in the direction of the vicarage.

❧

The Captain had been missing for days and Cherry let slip that he had walked to Kent, where a meeting of the Fancy was taking place for which the Captain had put up the purse. Sir Anthony could not but bemoan the fact he had not been invited and, indeed, he would have been most welcome, had he not been violently ill at the time that the Captain departed. The Captain had informed his hostess of his departure and promised to return by Wednesday, so Faith was comforted by the fact he had paid his hostess that civility, at least.

With the Captain gone Lord Frederick was temporarily stymied in his wish to ask for Faith's hand, but he meant to assure her, at least, that he had such an intention. However, he found that he could not persuade her to walk with him, or ride with him, or indeed spend any time alone with him whatsoever. When they reached the ruin, a most romantic aspect that Lord Frederick felt would lend itself to courtship, he found that Cherry stuck like a barnacle to her sister's side.

Both Cherry and Faith felt somewhat embarrassed at their lack of skill at sketching and, after walking twice around the grounds of the admittedly picturesque ruins, found little to do with themselves. Lydia and Lady Burke were quite talented, but the sisters could only admire their sketches for so long before that activity began to pall. Sir Anthony was also bored and wished he'd stayed behind to hunt with James; he had finally recovered from his previous indisposition and was tired of inactivity. However, he soon hit on a most ingenious scheme and approached Frederick where he sat with Cherry and Faith to tell him of it.

Frederick, however, had no desire to scale the walls of the ruin, not even for a bet, but Sir Anthony at least succeeded in interesting Cherry in the project, and Frederick was thrilled when Cherry left them and he could speak to Faith where no one could overhear.

Unfortunately, as soon as Cherry and Anthony left Faith got up to follow them, remembering her promise to her sister not to be alone with Lord Frederick.

"Faith, I mean, Miss Wentworth," Lord Frederick said, when he saw by her expression that his use of her first name provoked her displeasure, "why do you insist on avoiding me?"

Faith stopped at his statement, but did not look around. "I am not avoiding you, Lord Frederick, but I do not think it proper for us to be separated from the others."

"Please, Miss Wentworth, do not distrust me for my forward behavior of the other day. I meant you no insult. That is why I beg the honor of a few words with you out of the others' hearing. Indeed, if you look to your left you will see that we are still within sight of Lady Burke, should she look up from her sketching."

Faith thought perhaps she was being overly-cautious and Lord Frederick would think her foolish. He was not a monster, after all, and she found herself very curious to hear what he could have to say. So she turned back and walked over to where he stood, and waited expectantly for him to speak.

Frederick swallowed a few times, wondering why he hadn't thought this all out more clearly, but he finally managed a few words. "Faith, I have every intention of speaking to your father. I would have spoken to him before now, if he hadn't left so precipitously."

This speech caused all of Faith's doubts to come rushing back. He made no expression of admiration for her, but merely a determination to speak to her father. Could it be merely the game that caused him to want to win her hand?

"Please tell me something, Lord Frederick. I have heard there is a game in play that involves me. Is this true?"

Lord Frederick looked startled. "Who told you such a thing?"

Faith dismissed the question with a wave of her hand. "What does that matter? The only thing that matters is if it is true."

"I am not sure what exactly it is that you heard, but there is a reason behind it."

"So you admit there is a game?"

"Yes, but Faith, please permit me to explain—"

"I find that I'm not interested in your explanation, Lord Frederick. I thought you different from Sir Anthony, from my father, but it appears you're as irresponsible and light-minded as they are! Perhaps you're worse than them; you trifled with me and my affections, pretending you had feelings for me when you had none," she said, and Frederick felt a pang that she doubted the sincerity of his attentions, when his only goal had been to win her and her love. Indeed, he could see by her expression that she had been deeply hurt, and he cursed whoever had told her of the game.

"Faith, you do not understand! Your father was pressuring Sir Anthony to marry you and it was the only way I could stop the match from proceeding. I had no intention of trifling with your affections but of giving us both time to get to know each other better."

"I feel I do not know you at all," Faith said, and Lord Frederick felt an even deeper pang at her words.

"Then it is too early for me to speak," he said sadly, "but please tell me I do not hope in vain."

"What is it that you hope for, Lord Frederick?" Faith asked, though she told herself she was letting herself in for a severe disappointment should he verify he had no serious intentions toward her.

"Do you mean it is not obvious? I thought I wore my heart on my sleeve," he said with a bittersweet smile, holding his arm out and peering down at it, and Faith was reminded of their first meeting when she had said something similar to him. "I hope to win your hand, and your love," he told her, reaching out for her hand as he said it, before bringing it to his lips. "Please tell me I do not hope in vain?" he asked again, but Faith found it difficult to reassure him, as her own heart was beating so fiercely she found she could hardly think, or speak. She looked over to ensure that Lady Burke was still in sight, as she did not trust him, or perhaps herself, not to initiate another embrace.

Before she could reply, or remove her hand from his, they heard a woman's scream.

Fourteen

తురిం

Sir Anthony would never have imagined that he could enjoy a physical feat even more with a feminine companion than a masculine one, but he found Cherry very good company, indeed. His fellow sportsmen weren't inclined to look at him with admiring eyes, and he soon discovered that an appreciative look from Cherry was almost as motivating as a bet for spurring him on to greatness.

His goal was to climb about twenty feet up the side of one of the stone walls, and from there he would gain access to the church tower, which had steps that he could take to get down. There was no real reason for him to perform this feat other than boredom and rest-lessness, but Sir Anthony was relieved to discover Cherry had no desire to point this out to him, and entered into the spirit of the endeavor without the usual warnings and complaints he'd have heard from his mother or sisters. He showed her the indentations in the wall that he planned to use as footholds, and she listened carefully to his explanation.

"Sir Anthony, if you make it safely up the wall, do you think perhaps I could follow the same path? I dearly love a climb, and this looks as if it would be a jolly one."

Sir Anthony was not at all a spoilsport, and he

was also oblivious to social niceties when involved in one of his stunts, but even he recognized that Cherry's skirts might prove a hindrance to her on such a climb, so told her that unfortunately he could not advise such a thing.

"However, if you were to give me a ribbon, I will tie it at the top of the tower. Like a knight's token," he said, thrilled with himself for thinking of such a romantic gesture. It was too bad his mother, who felt he was such a failure at courtship, wasn't there to hear it. Then again, perhaps it was a good thing she was not present, as she would be sure to prevent him from performing his feat, and he checked again to ensure she could not see him from where she sat sketching.

Cherry blushingly complied with his request, removing the ribbon from her bonnet and shyly handing it to him. He grabbed her hand and brought it to his lips, and both felt the stunt had taken on the dimensions of a chivalrous task.

All proceeded as he could wish, and he was most of the way up and enjoying the climb, when he put his hand above him and the stone wall crumbled beneath his fingers. He was able to keep his balance and tried another spot but it, too, crumbled and Cherry, watching from below, cried out a warning: "Be careful, the wall is not secure at the top. Perhaps you should go no further.'

Sir Anthony had come to the same conclusion, but it was a lot easier to go up than it was to come down, and he was making his way very slowly back to the bottom when he slipped and Cherry screamed.

❧

Lord Frederick and Faith were the first to reach them, and Sir Anthony looked to be in a great deal of pain, holding his leg and trying not to curse.

"What happened?" Frederick asked, approaching Sir Anthony where he lay on the ground, Cherry at his side.

"I was trying to climb that blasted wall and slipped. I wasn't up high enough to do real damage, but I think I sprained my ankle."

"We'd better get you home. We'll have to drive your mother's gig and send back the carriage for her, as you cannot return the way you came."

Sir Anthony nodded but didn't speak again, as he was in a great deal of pain but didn't want to appear the complete weakling. His primary feeling was embarrassment that his gallant gesture had ended so ignominiously, and he couldn't meet Cherry's eyes. He realized he was still clutching her ribbon and, gritting his teeth, he said, "Here's your ribbon."

"Thank you," she said, taking it from his hand, and he was sure he could hear the disappointment in her voice.

Sir Anthony was correct that Cherry was disappointed, but wrong about the source of her disappointment. It was not his actions that caused it, but her own. She did not know what possessed her to *scream*, of all things! She had never done so before in her life, and she felt it was such a ridiculous, *feminine* thing to do. Sir Anthony was obviously quite disgusted with her and with good reason. So she made no attempt to speak to him further, or even to try to make him comfortable, as her sister did. She merely stood off to the side as he was helped into Lady Burke's gig and futilely wished she could turn back the clock and react to his fall in a manner that would not cause him to despise her.

৯৽৽৻

While all this was occurring Diana was starting on her course of self-improvement and piousness. As she began her morning by primping even longer in front of her mirror than usual in the desire to present an attractive appearance to Mr. Foster as she bared her soul to him, it is not to be feared that her feelings of remorse had crushed her personality to any significant degree.

Mr. Foster politely welcomed Miss Perrywhistle into his drawing room, apologizing for his sister's absence and asking Diana if she would like him to call the housekeeper.

"No! That is, if you do not mind, our privacy suits my purpose, as I have need of your advice as a spiritual counselor."

If Mr. Foster found it surprising that the worldly Miss Perrywhistle had sought him out on such an errand he hid his feelings well, merely inviting her to take a seat and asking in what manner he could serve her.

"I was very moved by your sermon yesterday, as it forced me to realize that I have been leading a very selfish, vain existence thus far. I would like to change my behavior but am not sure where to begin. I was hoping you could suggest a course of action."

As this admission resulted in Mr. Foster giving her a sample of the smile she desired to see above all others, Diana felt that her efforts at self-reformation

were already proving highly rewarding, and could not
wait to see Mr. Foster's expression when she actually
performed some good work at his suggestion. She only
hoped that he didn't expect her to begin that morning, as
her dress was far too nice to wear on a charitable mission. She was relieved when he didn't require her to dart
off immediately, and she listened attentively to his opinions on the education of the lower orders, thinking that
he had perhaps the most melodious voice she had ever
heard, and only interrupting him to comment that what
he said reminded her of a play she had seen once in
town, and asking him if he'd seen it before recounting
the plot to him.

When she finally left him some time later she
had agreed to make some charitable visits to the poor the
following day, and he had agreed to accompany her.
Truth be told, she was more excited at the prospect of
seeing him again than beginning the process of her reform, and devoted much of her time that afternoon to
the serious matter of what she should wear on the mor-
row. It needed to be suitably modest and demonstrate
she was serious-minded, but still attractive. She refused
to contemplate *why* it was she desired to attract Mr.
Foster.

She asked her maid Sally to help her modify one
of her dresses to fit the occasion, when she suddenly remembered Mr. Foster's speech on education for the
lower orders. Diana asked the girl if she could read, and
when she found she could not, asked her if she would
like to.

"Lawks! Why would I need to read, miss?" the
girl replied.

"I'm sure I don't know," Diana responded. "Forget that I mentioned it."

Thankfully for the poor little maidservant, who really did want to learn to read and had hoped to have her objection overturned, Diana later remembered one of the reasons Mr. Foster gave for being educated and mentioned it to Sally. At that point Sally was able to voice her true desire, and Diana nobly offered to spend some time each day teaching Sally to read.

Diana could hardly wait to tell Mr. Foster. Surely it would make him smile to hear it.

෴

After Sir Anthony had been safely ensconced in his bedchamber, his foot propped up and the doctor called, Lady Burke returned downstairs to report on his progress. Faith and Cherry were waiting in the drawing room, and Lady Burke greeted them with a tsk of annoyance.

"That son of mine! When will he grow up? I try to be patient with him but, really! What a stupid lark to embark on, with no consideration for the consequences to himself and others!"

She continued in this manner for a few minutes, having been shaken out of her normal placid demeanor by the events of the morning and her sincere concern for her son. Faith listened to her hostess's complaints in sympathy and understanding, as she entertained the same sentiments, thinking Sir Anthony immature and selfish and very like her father in his addiction to sport and games. She was not his mother, however, so while she nodded and murmured her agreement, she made no accusations of her own.

Cherry, on the other hand, while concerned for Sir Anthony, was not at all inclined to criticize him for his morning's actions, and could not sit still for long while another did so. She tried to keep silent but self-control did not come easily to her, and so sat fuming until she could take it no longer. As Lady Burke had finally finished with her complaints and begun a different subject, she was surprised when Cherry interrupted her to cry passionately, "You do not understand!"

Lady Burke did *not* understand, as she had merely asked if the girls had eaten and said that, if not, there was some cold meat set out in the dining room. Faith, however, who had been observing Cherry apprehensively during Lady Burke's diatribe, knew to what Cherry referred and so told her sister, "Cherry, it is none of your affair!"

However, the floodgates had been opened and Lady Burke was not left long in ignorance of Cherry's true feelings. "I beg your pardon, Lady Burke, but I cannot sit idly by while you attack Sir Anthony's character. You truly do not understand him, just as Faith has never understood our father! Have you never felt the satisfaction of pitting your strength against an obstacle, and then feeling yourself overcome it? The point is not in reaching the destination, but in undertaking the voyage. To feel your heart pound and your muscles contract, to know that you, a puny combination of flesh and blood, cannot be constrained by your body but can be the master of it! It is of all feelings the best and most exhilarating. It is far more thrilling than sitting in a chair knitting a fringe, or reading in a book of another's exploits. And I only wish I had been born a man, so that I could have joined Sir Anthony in climbing that rock wall today. Instead, to think I failed him with my feminine weakness—" she broke off at this point and ran from the room, ignoring Lady Burke's call for her to stay.

Lady Burke and Faith looked at each other speechlessly for a moment, before Lady Burke asked, "Feminine weakness?"

"I believe she must mean when she screamed. I know she frequently calls such behavior missish and affected."

"Ah, I see." Lady Burke was silent for a moment more, and then sighed. "She is right to some extent; I truly do not understand Sir Anthony's taste for sports. His father was not at all like him."

"What sort of gentleman was he?"

"The best sort," Lady Burke said, with a fond smile. "Anthony does resemble his father in that he is kind and equitable, but Sir John was a good deal older than me, and when Anthony left the nursery his father was past the age of sports. I wonder sometimes if that is not why Anthony embraced them so vigorously."

"That does not explain why *Cherry* does so. She is a lady, however much she'd wish it otherwise."

"Perhaps, if she continues to spend time with my son, she'll cease to wish for such a thing."

Faith wondered if she correctly understood Lady Burke's meaning, and looked at the older lady for a moment before replying. She was relieved to see Lady Burke was smiling, if rather wryly. "I assume you've noticed her partiality for Sir Anthony?" Faith asked.

"It's difficult to miss, but she is still very young. It may all come to nothing," Lady Burke said. "I must confess, that when you all first arrived, I had hoped Sir Anthony would one day introduce *you* as my daughter-in-law."

Faith smiled warmly at Lady Burke. "I would have gladly embraced such a role. If one were to marry for the sake of a mother- in-law, a match with Sir Anthony could not have pleased me more."

"But then you found you favored Lord Frederick?"

Faith's smile disappeared and she looked at Lady Burke in surprise. "Whatever do you mean?"

"I am sorry, my dear, if I am being too officious, it is no affair of mine, after all. However, I have noticed that you two appear to display a—preference for each other."

"No, Lady Burke, you are not being officious. I have longed to discuss the matter with you. I just had not supposed my feelings so transparent," Faith said, embarrassed.

"They are not, my dear. Actually, it was very difficult for me to read your feelings, at first. That is why I hoped, until just recently, that you might make a match with Anthony. But the past few days it has been a little more obvious to me that there is *something* between you and Lord Frederick. And while I'm still unsure if you return his regard, it's apparent that Lord Frederick is greatly enamored of you."

"*Is* it apparent, my lady?" Faith asked, a little wistfully. "Could not love be just another game, to a sportsman?"

"Not if he calls himself a gentleman! And I have known Lord Frederick since he was a boy. He's a good man, Faith, and not the sort to toy with a young lady's affections. I've never seen him seriously court any young lady. No, as much as I hate to give you up," she said with a smile, "I must admit that it would be a good match."

"I just find it so difficult to entrust my happiness to *any* gentleman. For most of my life I have not found much to admire in them, and much to abhor."

Lady Burke got up from where she was sitting and joined Faith on the sofa, taking one of her hands in hers. "My poor child, you've been sadly neglected, haven't you? And it's an unfortunate truth that many men are self-absorbed and neglectful of their wives. *I* was very fortunate in that Sir John treated me with much indulgence. I would imagine Lord Frederick would treat you similarly, but it might be a good idea if you were to ask him his views on marriage."

"*Ask* him?"

"Why not? Like I said, he's a good man, and I'm confident he'll give you an honest response. And it's good to hash all these things out. But maybe you just need to know him a little better. It takes time to build trust, you know."

Faith was reminded of a similar conversation she'd had with Lord Frederick, but before she could reply Cherry had re-entered the drawing room and walked over to the sofa, taking a position in front of Lady Burke, her eyes downcast.

"Lady Burke, I must ask your forgiveness. I should not have spoken to you as I did," she said, a little stiffly, as if she had memorized the words in her bed-chamber prior to entering the saloon.

"My dear child," Lady Burke exclaimed, jumping up to take Cherry's hands in hers, "you do not need to apologize. You were quite right to explain matters to me. I had no idea, you see, that climbing a rock wall was such a noble endeavor."

Cherry raised her eyes to look suspiciously at Lady Burke, convinced that she was teasing her, which she was, a little. However, Lady Burke smile was very sincere and tender and Cherry did have a sense of humor, so she smiled back at Lady Burke. "Perhaps it's not exactly *noble*, but it is great fun."

"I'm sure it is, and I will try to be patient with you and Sir Anthony's enthusiasm for it if you'll be patient with my desire to knit a fringe."

Cherry agreed, smiling, but her smile faded a little as she thought again about poor Sir Anthony, confined to his room and unable to participate in the activities he held so dear. She mentioned as much to Lady Burke.

"Then, my dear, you must undertake to entertain him."

"How? I cannot walk or ride with him, or play billiards with him, in the condition he's in now."

"Perhaps you could converse with him," Faith suggested.

"About what?" Cherry looked truly puzzled.

"Can you not find a subject to discuss?" Faith asked, exasperated with her sister.

"I don't think he would wish to talk to me, after I made such a fool of myself this morning."

"Perhaps you could start by discussing that," Lady Burke suggested.

"And I could read to him from the *Sporting Magazine*, and we can play cards for a penny a point," she said exultantly, and Lady Burke and Faith exchanged a dismayed look. It appeared Cherry was not to be led into serious subjects very easily.

Their conversation was interrupted at that point by the arrival of the doctor, so Lady Burke left them to go to her son's side, promising to return later to tell them his prognosis.

Fifteen

❧

Sir Anthony was ordered to stay off of his ankle for three days, but could begin to resume some of his normal activities at the end of the week. Three days of inactivity sounded an interminable period to the sports mad young gentleman, but his mother had told him that Miss Cherry proposed to help entertain him, and he cheered up slightly, relieved that he had not totally disgraced himself in her eyes.

The program for his entertainment, however, was not to begin until the following afternoon, as his mother felt it wiser for him to have undisturbed rest that first day and she was taking the young ladies shopping the next morning. Lady Burke was determined to introduce Cherry to *some* feminine pursuits, and so had invited her and Faith to accompany her to her dressmaker's.

Diana and Lydia were also invited but Diana turned down the invitation. She was oddly absent much of the time during the day, but when she was present at dinner Faith found her far more approachable than before. Lord Frederick, too, felt much more at ease in Diana's company now that she'd ceased trying to flirt with him. Of course, if Faith would try such a thing he'd have no objection in the least.

He agonized over how he could win her trust, and told himself yet again that time was necessary. She was still shy with him, but was no longer avoiding him like she had been doing the first few days after he had kissed her. And he was greatly encouraged when they gathered in the drawing room after dinner and she agreed to play chess with him.

He knew her to be a good chess player, but this evening it seemed as if her mind was not on the game. When it was her turn she stared at the pieces for longer than usual without making a move, before commenting, "Lord Frederick, many chess players find the Queen to be the most valuable piece on the board. Would you agree?"

"Yes, of course. Are you trying to distract me so that you can capture her from me?"

"I just find it interesting, how high a position this woman holds," Faith touched her Queen briefly with a finger, "when real women have no power at all."

"Behind that modest exterior do you secretly yearn to be the next Boadicea?" Lord Frederick asked her.

"No, of course not. I am not ambitious, socially or politically, as you might have guessed. However, I do wonder what position you feel a woman should hold in her own household," Faith said, a little hesitantly. She was trying to take Lady Burke's advice but found it difficult to ask how she would be treated as his wife when she had not even been formally offered that position, and was still unsure whether she even wanted it. She could no longer meet his eyes as she awaited his response, and looked down at the board as if trying to determine what her next move should be.

"She has a very important position. Mother to

her children, confidant to her husband," Lord Frederick replied, though he felt it was a poor sort of answer. He believed Faith was testing him and wished so hard to pass he was too nervous for eloquence.

She looked up at him with a shy smile, and Frederick was slightly reassured. He must have answered correctly. "Confidant?" she asked him. "So in your view, a married couple should confide in each other, as friends would?"

"Exactly. They should be the best of friends."

"And if the couple had a difference of opinion?"

"Well, I suppose they should talk it over."

"So a wife's opinion, in your view, should bear weight with her husband?"

"Of course. He should value her opinion above all others."

"That's quite radical of you, Lord Frederick. I doubt many men would reply similarly."

"They are fools then. If they choose a woman to be the mother of their children, it is to be hoped they would trust her opinion."

"Even though she has not been educated as a man has?"

"I don't think a classical education necessarily ensures wisdom, or even intelligence. Did you read Wollstonecraft, then?"

"Yes, though I have not yet finished. But I do agree that a woman has a purpose in life other than that of merely making herself agreeable to a man. I think it rather vain of men to assume such a thing," Faith said, and looked at Lord Frederick as if daring him to disagree with her.

"Men are vain creatures, my dear," he said, smiling. "However, you do have a powerful weapon, as Rosseau pointed out. You can use your feminine wiles to twist us men around your finger."

"I would not know how to do such a thing, nor would I want to. It sounds manipulative and deceitful," Faith said.

"I would not like to be manipulated, it's true, but love exerts its own influence, wouldn't you agree?"

"So if a man truly loves his wife, and she him, your argument is that they would want to please each other," Faith said.

"In every way," Lord Frederick said softly, and Faith blushed, though she was not sure why. She supposed it was the intimate tone in which he said it. She looked down at the board, wondering if it was still her turn. Before she could ask, Lord Frederick said, "Your move, Faith."

She did not think he was referring merely to the chess game.

❧❦

Captain Wentworth returned to the house party on Wednesday afternoon to find his youngest daughter in the drawing room playing backgammon with Sir Anthony, who had his foot propped up on a cushion. Lady Burke and Mrs. Perrywhistle were also present, seated by the window doing needlework, but there was no sign of the other members of the party.

"Captain Wentworth, how good to have you back! You can tell us about the prizefight," Sir Anthony said, sitting up straighter on the sofa.

"Yes, Papa, who won the purse?" Cherry asked him eagerly.

Captain Wentworth was unsure which annoyed him more: Cherry's question or the sight of Sir Anthony lying on a sofa in the middle of the day. He'd seemed such a promising young man, the Captain had had high hopes for him, but he was turning out to be a huge disappointment.

"What is the matter, Sir Anthony? You can't mean to say you've been down since our little bit of training last week?" the Captain asked him, and Lady Burke heaved a sigh of relief that she wouldn't be called on to change the subject. For no discussion of a prizefight would be had in her hearing in a polite drawing room.

"No, of course not. That was no more than a temporary indisposition. This was caused by a fall I took on Monday—" Sir Anthony began.

"It was not his fault, Papa, truly. The wall was crumbling at the top and he had climbed twenty feet at least before it became apparent it would not hold him."

This remark changed the frown on the Captain's face to a grin, and he found himself in charity with Sir Anthony once again. "Say no more, I perceive exactly how it was, young man. A wager, I gather. Ah, well, these things can't be helped. The number of injuries I've sustained—but then, I'm never down for long. It's the diet, you see. It makes all the difference."

Sir Anthony didn't appear heartened to hear this, as he had grown to despise the Captain's dietary advice and he could feel his stomach turn at the mere thought of it. So he just nodded as the Captain expounded the benefits of a plain diet and purging, and hoped the others could not hear the gurgling of his stomach

Thankfully the Captain could not be kept inside for long and, after promising Sir Anthony he'd tell him all about the prize match after dinner that evening, excused himself to the ladies and left. Sir Anthony couldn't help but notice how depressed Cherry was that her father would not tell her the details of the fight, so after his mother resumed her sewing Anthony whispered in Cherry's ear, "I'll tell you all about it, afterward."

His reward was such a glowing smile from Cherry that he once again felt he'd performed some knight-errantry, and wondered how his mother could have ever questioned his ability with the ladies. It was obvious he was a nonpareil in that regard.

❧

Sir Anthony had reason to wish his ankle to heal quickly, as there was a fete planned for the servants that Saturday, and while the games and prizes were ostensibly for them, Sir Anthony could never restrain himself from taking part. Indeed, he invariably won whichever game he participated in, but as it was a source of pride to the servants that their master was not one of your effeminate noble weaklings, they expected and enjoyed his participation.

Cherry heard about the fair from Sir Anthony and secretly determined that she would participate as well. Finding herself quite in sympathy with her sister these days, she even ventured to confide her plans to

Faith.

Faith heard her without comment, although she was tempted to voice her disapproval. She was relieved, however, to find that Cherry merely intended to participate in the archery contest, and didn't intend to climb a greasy pole for a flitch of bacon or engage in some other activity completely unsuitable for a female.

Seeing her sister's dislike of the scheme written on her face, Cherry hurried to tell her, "Sir Anthony said his sisters have participated in the archery contest in the past."

This did relieve Faith's mind, but recently she had wished she understood her sister better and thought this might be a good time to discover what was behind Cherry's interest in sports. "I am sure, then, there can be no objection to your participation, but I wonder, Cherry, why it is that you *want* to participate."

"It is hard to explain, Faith. I suppose it is because I feel that I am just as good at these things as a man, and I hate to be dismissed as of no account by them because of the fact that I was born female. Why should men treat us as inferior beings when we can do whatever they can do, and sometimes we can even do it better?"

Faith wondered if this was her sister's reaction to the neglect they'd experienced since they were children. It was true that Cherry had always received a great deal of attention because of her unladylike behavior, and while it was generally negative, perhaps she felt that it had been better than being ignored. Faith, while having no desire to compete with men on a physical level, did not at all appreciate being treated as an inferior and could fully comprehend her sister's feelings.

"I have never tried archery, but it looks as if it would be fun. Maybe you can show me how it's done?" Faith asked her sister.

Cherry looked surprised, then giggled. "And set you up as my competitor? That would be very foolish of me."

"Cherry," Faith said, sounding like her old bossy self.

"Oh, very well. I suppose it would be even more of a comeuppance to those uppity males if *two* ladies show themselves to be worthy opponents."

❧❦

However, after one afternoon at archery Faith was not sure she'd be able to compete in the contest, much to her dismay, for she found she enjoyed archery very much, and therein lay the problem.

After Cherry had given her some simple instruction and left her, Faith devoted the rest of the afternoon to practice, only to find that archery used muscles heretofore not introduced into the world. By the time she stopped an hour later she found that her hand was shaking, and as the day progressed her arm and shoulder were so weak as to be useless.

She was extremely embarrassed. After all her strictures about others' foolish devotion to sport, she had injured herself in her enthusiasm for archery.

Faith retired to her room before dinner, certain if she rested for an hour or so she'd regain the use of her arm. However, by the time she went down to the drawing room her arm was still far too weak to use, and it ached abominably. She thought about giving her excuses but did not wish to draw attention to her silly injury. She was hopeful she could hide it from the others.

She was successful at first, as she gave her left arm to Lord Frederick when he escorted her into dinner and her right was the one giving her pain. But she soon discovered it was too painful to hold her fork in her right hand and so switched to her left. She did not think Lord Frederick would notice such a small thing, but he did almost immediately.

"You are using your left hand to eat tonight, I see. Is something the matter with your right?"

"It's rather silly. I spent the afternoon at archery and as it was the first time I've engaged in the sport, I seem to have strained my muscles a trifle."

Faith was dismayed to find there was a pause in the other diner's conversation just as she made her confession and, though she spoke very softly, Cherry and her father overheard.

"Faith! I told you not to practice too long your first time," Cherry said.

"I know, Cherry, you were right. I should have heeded your advice. Believe me, I wish I had."

"It is just as I've always said: Women are too weak physically to participate in sport," Captain Wentworth proclaimed.

There were instant outcries from Cherry, and Faith also joined in the protest, as she knew she'd disappointed her sister by confirming their father's opinion of the "weaker" sex.

However, it was Lord Frederick who made himself heard. "I beg your pardon, Captain, but that's non-sense! I am sure it is just as Miss Wentworth said, she has strained a muscle from overuse. The same thing could happen to a man just as easily."

There was a moment's silence, and then the Captain surprised everyone by smiling. "I suppose, female or male, you've come by it honestly. It's rather a relief to find that your mother didn't play me false." The Captain laughed uproariously at this, though Faith didn't find it all that funny a supposition. "Though you'd do better to save that arm for your sewing," Faith's father advised her.

The conversation turned general once again, and Faith turned to Lord Frederick, smiling at him in grati-tude for his intervention. "Shall you save your arm for sewing?" Lord Frederick asked Faith.

She considered it a moment, then told him, "You know, I find I enjoy archery far more."

"Perhaps when your arm heals we can shoot to-gether."

"I would enjoy that," Faith told him. "Though I think it should be a *short* game."

"Agreed," Lord Frederick said.

Later that evening when the gentlemen rejoined the ladies in the drawing room after dinner, Lord Freder-ick sat out from the card games to keep Faith company on the sofa. She protested, sure that he would find it dull by her side.

"I can just go up to my room, Lord Frederick. You need not sacrifice your pleasure for my sake," Faith told him.

"You do not seem to understand; I do not consider having you all to myself in the nature of a sacrifice but rather as a reward."

"You are very gallant, Lord Frederick."

"I hope so, but in this case I am merely following my own inclination. I *enjoy* your company, Faith. There is no one I'd rather be with this evening, or any other. And the only thing that would bring me greater joy is to hear you feel likewise."

This was plain speaking, indeed. Faith lowered her eyes in embarrassment, but Frederick put a finger under her chin and raised her face so that her eyes met his. He was almost sorry he did so, because he lost track of the conversation when exposed to her gaze. In the candlelight it was hard to make out her expression, but surely there was affection hidden in the shadowed depths of her eyes? Surely she must return his feelings? When she finally spoke he was too distracted at first to comprehend her words.

"I do feel likewise," she had said, very softly, and when he finally took in the meaning of her words his heart jumped in his chest. "But," she continued, "it is such a leap of faith, is it not? To put your heart in another's keeping? How can I know it will be safe?"

Frederick warned himself again to go slowly. He was far too precipitous, and right now, if he followed his inclination to pull Faith in his arms, he'd shock not only his beloved but also all the inhabitants of the drawing room, who were out of earshot but still within view. "It *is* a leap of faith, but not just for you. You remember the old proverb: 'In wedding and all things to look ere ye leap'? That was written to advise gentlemen to be careful in selecting a wife. I, too, have a heart that is vulnerable.

But I've looked very carefully, and am willing to take that leap. I must assume, however, that you do not like what you've seen of *my* character."

"No, no, that is not true! You are all that is honorable and kind! The problem is in me, as I've told you before. I find it difficult to trust. But as to *liking*, there is no question of that. I like you very much, indeed."

Damned with faint praise, Frederick thought to himself. It was obvious by Faith's expression that she thought she'd bestowed quite the encomium. Her eyes were glowing with...like? Surely there was something stronger there than that! Frederick grabbed her left hand and brought it to his lips. "I am relieved to find you like me, Faith. But I hope for much more than that. However, I will wait until you are sure of your feelings. Indeed, I have no choice," he said, a little wryly.

Faith was conscious of the fact that she'd disappointed him, though it had taken all of her courage to proclaim she liked him. Surely he did not expect a declaration of love, and they not even engaged! And she was still unsure if she *did* love him. She was happier in his company than in anyone else's, and when she was away from him she found herself counting the minutes until she could see him again, but she still found herself terrified at the thought of committing herself so irrevocably to a man.

Faith was distracted from her musings, however, by the fact that he still held her hand lightly clasped in his. She looked over at the card players, but they all seemed engrossed in their game, and none appeared to notice Lord Frederick's possession of her hand.

"What were the words of the ballad you were

singing when we first arrived?" Lord Frederick asked, as
he played with the fingers of her left hand.

"Umm, the ballad…You mean, 'Oh, let the night
my blushes hide'?" Faith asked, thankful that those
words proved true right now, and that her blushes were
concealed in the candlelight.

"Yes, that is the one. How did the second stanza
go?" Frederick released Faith's hand, and she was unsure
if she were more relieved or disappointed. But after resting his hand for a moment on the back of the sofa, he
began busying it again with playing in the curls at the
base of her neck.

"The second stanza?" Faith asked, unsure what it
was they were discussing. She struggled to ignore the
nervous fluttering in her stomach as his fingers lightly
caressed her neck and shoulders, trying to concentrate on
his question. Finally, she was able to sing softly:

But must we wait till age and care
Shall fix our wedding day;
How can his eyes so much declare,
His tongue so little say?"

"Not only a pretty tune, but it expresses my feelings exactly, were you to change the pronoun to the
feminine gender," Lord Frederick said when she'd completed her song. "Faith, I will try to content myself with
what your eyes say, for they speak volumes. Unless I
misread them?" Lord Frederick asked, his own eyes sending a potent message.

"No, I think you have interpreted their meaning
correctly," she managed to say, and when he smiled at

her, she knew that this time she had not disappointed him.

Sixteen
❧❧

Diana was finding Mr. Foster an even more re-
calcitrant suitor than Lord Frederick was finding Faith.
She had spent almost every day in his company this past
week, and discovered that none of her flirtatious glances
or witticisms had the least effect on him. He merely
looked at her with that enigmatic glance that she was
sure penetrated her stylish façade and saw through to the
real Diana. So she had concentrated instead on trying to
win smiles from him. She had proved so successful at
her second endeavor that she had lost count of the number of smiles she had received. Still, it seemed not to
matter how many she was granted; each one continued to
have the same unsettling effect on her equilibrium.

She was also surprised at how much she'd enjoyed the time they spent together in charitable works.
It was not at all boring, as she had feared; she had found
herself far more bored at some of the society functions
she'd attended in town. And when her maid successfully
read her first sentence Diana could have shouted for joy
and triumph, and had to content herself with grabbing
Sally's hands and dancing around the room.

Mr. Foster and his sister were to dine that evening at Kenilworth, and Diana was a little worried at
meeting him again in the others' company. She could
not endure it if he were to proffer that smile just as

freely to another lady. She'd far rather keep him and his smiles to herself.

The Captain had been distracted with a pursuit of his own that had caused him to temporarily forget the reason he'd come to Kenilworth, but when he saw Mr. Foster at dinner that evening he was reminded of the need to tie up the loose strings of his elder daughter's life. When the ladies left the gentlemen to their port he wasted no time at all getting to the heart of the matter.

"So, Foster's here. Are we ready to conclude this matter, Sir Anthony? Maybe you want to take a swig of brandy to brace your nerves. I'm sure it wouldn't hurt this once," the Captain said, and Sir Anthony began to wonder why he had wished so heartily for the Captain's presence, as it appeared he was never again to be able to enjoy a glass of brandy without the Captain's permission.

Before Sir Anthony could speak and, indeed, he was not in a hurry to do so, James Perrywhistle spoke up. "You can count me out. I've been utterly defeated. Can't seem to get my head back into the game. Just freeze up every time."

He continued mumbling under his breath, something about "eyes" and "smiles", but the gentlemen were distracted by Mr. Foster's entry into the conversation.

"I am no longer a disinterested observer, so cannot continue to offer my services as referee," he announced, and there was a shocked silence following his remark.

"The game is forfeit!" the Captain shouted, though he was unsure if this development would prove to be good or bad. He could scarcely remember why they had embarked on the game, and only knew Sir Anthony was supposed to have answered some questions before proposing to Faith. It seemed a silly thing in Captain Wentworth's opinion, but if Sir Anthony wanted to answer questions the Captain could ask him a few about his annual income and holdings before handing Faith over to him, and everything would be settled quite nicely, in his opinion.

Frederick wondered at Mr. Foster's announcement. He hoped that it did not mean the Vicar was interested in Faith though, if he was, Frederick had no doubt Foster was bound for disappointment. Frederick was confident of Faith's affections, and was sure she did not spare the Vicar more than a passing thought. But he found it hard to believe Foster would have made such a statement if he did not have some assurance the object of his interest returned his regard and Frederick wondered who the lady might be. (Though he was so far from suspecting it could be Diana Perrywhistle that if someone had ventured to suggest it was she, he would have laughed aloud at the thought.)

Sir Anthony was waiting for Lord Frederick to rise to the occasion, and was stymied when no additional announcements took place and the Captain continued to gaze at him expectantly. "Um, Lord Frederick, I believe you had something you wanted to say to the Captain?" Sir Anthony prompted him.

"I can wait my turn. I supposed you had something to say first."

"Yes, of course," Sir Anthony said, with a glare at his friend, who had apparently decided to wait until Sir Anthony disavowed any interest in the young lady before he spoke to her father. "Well, then, Captain, perhaps you'd like to join me in my study?"

The interview that followed was enjoyed by neither Sir Anthony nor Captain Wentworth, who felt he'd been invited to Kenilworth under false pretenses and threatened to leave the next day with both his daughters. However, he immediately remembered he had a favor to beg of Sir Anthony and was forced to retract his hasty words.

"These things happen, I suppose, though I don't think it very sporting of you to lead my daughter to form expectations, but least said soonest mended, what? I wouldn't want to leave too hastily and give rise to gossip."

Sir Anthony, who would not have been too disappointed to see the back of a most troublesome guest, was obliged to assure him that he and his family were welcome to stay as long as they liked. Before the Captain could bring up the project that was even dearer to his heart than marrying off his daughter, there was a knock at the door and Lord Frederick begged the pleasure of a few words with Captain Wentworth.

"Of course, Lord Frederick, please come in," Sir Anthony said, relieved he'd be able to make his escape. "I will rejoin the ladies and await you both in the drawing room."

"Just a moment, Sir Anthony," the Captain said, but Anthony had already shut the door behind him. The Captain wondered what bad news Lord Frederick might have for him and sat down with a grunt. "What is it, Lord Frederick?"

"Sir, you would do me the greatest honor if you would give me leave to pay my addresses to Miss Wentworth."

"What? *You*, pay your addresses to my daughter? What the deuce? Ah, I think I begin to understand. You came up with that nonsensical game to prevent Sir Anthony from coming up to scratch. Very wily of you, I must say." The Captain had no objection to wily behavior in the pursuit of a win and was not overly concerned which gentleman married his daughter, as long as he was a man of substance, which he knew Lord Frederick to be. He verified this suspicion by asking Lord Frederick a number of questions concerning his income and situation, which Lord Frederick had expected and was able to answer to the Captain's satisfaction.

"Well, then, Lord Frederick, you've got my permission; now it just remains for you to get the young lady's. But I fancy a crafty young gentleman like you is already pretty certain of the gel," the Captain said, winking and giving Lord Frederick a playful shove that almost knocked him over.

Lord Frederick rubbed his shoulder and hoped his new wife would not desire to visit her father too frequently after their marriage. "You can never be too certain when a lady is involved, Captain," Lord Frederick told him, then hurriedly left the Captain to join the ladies.

∂∞∕

Diana Perrywhistle was quite pleased when Mr. Foster came to her side as soon as he entered the drawing room, but she was determined not to be tricked a second time into thinking he did so because he desired her company. So she finished her song and looked up at him as he stood by the pianoforte, asking him, "Is the candelabra placed in the appropriate position, Mr. Foster? We would not want the draperies catching on fire."

"Yes, Miss Perrywhistle. The candelabra is perfectly situated. Your face is lit most enchantingly."

"You speak as if that was my intention in placing it there, though you must know I could not have managed such a thing by design."

"Miss Perrywhistle, it is my belief that there is no deed of which you're not capable."

Diana did not know whether he meant this as a compliment or an insult. He could be accusing her of being a designing female which, of course, she was. And, truth be told, she chose her position at the pianoforte and even the placement of the candelabra in order to present the most attractive picture possible when he entered the room. She studied him warily for a moment, wondering if he had indeed uncovered her schemes, unsure how to respond. He was the only person in the world who ever caused Diana to be at a loss for words.

And then he smiled at her. And once more she found words highly overrated.

"Will you come to the library with me?" Mr. Foster asked, and Diana nodded and rose to follow him out of the room, telling her mother that she was going to retrieve a book from the library for Mr. Foster. Her mother nodded absently, but Lydia stared at her sister as if she'd suddenly sprouted horns. Diana quit the saloon as quickly as she could, before Lydia or James could comment on her odd behavior.

She felt her heart racing as she walked beside Mr.

Foster down the darkened halls, wondering what he might have to say to her when they reached the library. Was she finally to have him in her thrall? Had she successfully captured his heart? It hardly seemed possible, but she'd never tried so hard to win anyone's approval. Surely her efforts had borne fruit.

He requested her to sit on the sofa, then took a position in front of her. He did not smile but looked quite solemn, and Diana felt her hopes fading in the face of his dour expression.

"Miss Perrywhistle, I do not think it wise for us to continue to spend so much time together. I believe it would be best if we only saw each other in company."

Diana was horrified. This was the opposite of what she had expected. What was she to do if she could no longer see him? She had finally felt she had a purpose in life. He could not take that away from her! He could not take *himself* away from her. "I do not understand what you mean. We have accomplished so many good things, why should we stop?"

"I feel that I cannot in honor spend so much time with you, when recently I find myself overwhelmed with the desire to kiss you."

"You do?" Diana asked, her slightly undersized eyes widening until they were a most attractive size.

"And you would never permit such a thing."

"No, of course not," she said, trying to sound firm, though even to her own ears it sounded a very weak denial.

"No, for you are leagues above me. I could never hope to win your heart, your hand. You would not be content with the life I could offer you. So I am afraid we must part."

"Must we?" Diana said, wondering how she could change the course of this interview. "Mr. Foster, perhaps I could be allowed to speak for myself, for I do not think you've read my character at all accurately."

"Have I not? Then of course you should tell me where I've erred. May I be allowed to sit?" he asked, placing himself beside her on the sofa.

"It was all untrue, all of it!" Diana said, flustered by his nearness. He smiled at her, and she was lost.

"Perhaps we should begin with the first point and proceed from there. It is not true, then, that you would never permit me to kiss you?" Mr. Foster asked, putting his arms around her.

"I am sorry to contradict you, sir, but you could not be more mistaken," Diana said, leaning in for his kiss.

❧

Faith did not like to admit, even to herself, that she had kept a close eye on the door, eagerly awaiting Lord Frederick's entrance. She had refused to join in a card game preferring to sit alone and read, though her book did not keep her full attention. She found herself frequently looking up at the door and wondered, after Sir Anthony's entrance, why Lord Frederick still had not come. She also wondered if it could have anything to do with her father's absence, but did not feel it wise to speculate about the circumstance, which was bound to be purely coincidental.

When Lord Frederick did at last enter and his

eyes immediately found hers, she saw such a glowing look of happiness and ardor that she found herself growing excited as well, though she did not know the cause. Or perhaps she did know, and would shortly be free to admit it. For of course no lady could ever reveal her own feelings until the gentleman had declared himself, first.

He strode to her side, offering her his arm. "Miss Wentworth, you appear slightly flushed. Would you care to step outside for a breath of air?"

Mrs. Perrywhistle, who was generally as mute as a mouse, made herself heard at a most unpropitious time, in Lord Frederick's view. "Walk outside at this hour?" she exclaimed, looking up from her needlework. "Oh, no, I'm afraid it would be most ill-advised! The night air is highly insalubrious. My doctor always advises me to stay inside after sunset."

"Perhaps that is true for you, Mrs. Perrywhistle, but Miss Wentworth is so young and healthy. I am sure a few minutes in the night air will not harm her. That is, if you're sure her father would permit it, Lord Frederick," Lady Burke said, with a significant look at the young gentleman.

"Indeed, I have already sought and received her father's consent to our stroll," Lord Frederick said, and escorted Faith from the room before anyone else could prevent their departure.

Once he had achieved his goal, however, he was unsure exactly how to proceed, and his companion's shyness did not aid matters. She would not meet his glance until finally he said, "Faith, darling, won't you even look at me?"

At that she did look up and Lord Frederick, struck anew by her delicate beauty, forgot that he had not yet spoken and took her in his arms instead. He was surprised that she would not submit to his embrace, but instead pushed against his chest and turned her face away from his.

"Faith, why will you not let me kiss you? Don't you know how much I adore you?" he murmured, grabbing the hands pressed against his chest and dropping kisses on them.

"How would I know, Lord Frederick, when you have not yet told me?" Faith said, though she stopped her struggles and stood, unresisting, in his embrace.

"Oh, Faith, how impetuous and stupid I am, have always been, with you," he told her, lifting her up and swinging her around in circles until she giggled, convinced somehow that no matter how oddly he'd set about it, this was to end in a marriage proposal.

"I love you, dear girl, and want nothing more than to spend the rest of my life with you. I should mention, too, that your father has given his consent to our marriage."

"Has he, indeed? Were you and Sir Anthony forced to draw straws for the honor, or did you lose to him in a wager?"

"I'll have you know that I have been in love with you almost from the moment I saw you in town."

"No! Is that true? And here I thought it was my gracefulness on our walk in the gardens that won you over."

"Your lack of grace at that moment was a deciding factor, it's true. You are free to fall into my arms at any and every opportunity," Frederick told her, before growing serious. "Dearest, loveliest Faith. Will you marry me?"

Faith also grew serious, and Frederick became concerned that he'd rejoiced too soon and she was going to refuse him. She placed one small hand against his cheek, took a deep breath, and asked him, "And if I say yes, what will our life together be?"

"It will be wonderful. For if I become too impetuous I'll have you by my side to check me, and if you become overcautious I'll be there to remind you 'nothing ventured, nothing gained,' and of other pithy sayings that support my point of view."

Faith laughed at this and he dropped a brief kiss on her lips before continuing. "And we will have beautiful baby girls that look like their mother and that you will teach to be dignified and sweet, and handsome boys that will grow up to be athletic and strong like their grandfather, with a leavening dose of common sense, inherited from their father."

"Will you subscribe to the *Sporting Magazine*?"

"I already do. But I promise to only read you the jokes, and only if they are good."

"And you must promise only to tell them once. I find even a good joke doesn't bear repeated telling."

"I promise. Is that your only request? Because I think most young ladies in your position would bargain for a jewel or two or a wedding trip to Paris."

"Could you afford it? If so, and a trip to Paris is in the offing, it would be foolish of me to decline. I've always longed to travel."

"I know. And I'd be more than pleased to take

you anywhere you'd like to go. But first you must accept me."

"I think I must," Faith said, and Frederick took this odd reply as an acceptance and bent again to kiss her lips. He soon found he'd wasted too much time talking, as his beloved was obviously far more pleased by actions than words. He would have spent even longer attempting to convince her had not Cherry come out of the house to tell them Mrs. Perrywhistle was concerned about Faith catching cold.

As Cherry glared at Lord Frederick as she said this, he was relieved when Faith told her immediately, "Cherry, you must be the first to congratulate us."

"Really? You are to marry him, then? What a relief. I must tell Sir Anthony," Cherry said, before submitting to the embrace to which Faith subjected her. However, Cherry soon unbent enough to congratulate her new prospective brother-in-law and ask when and where the wedding would be.

"We are not sure; we have not had time to talk about it," Frederick said, and Faith was more than satisfied with his reply, having half expected him to make a decision without consulting her wishes. She was relieved to see that her trust in him was not misplaced. She had still had misgivings when she had first ventured outside with him but had allowed him to sweep her off her feet, literally and figuratively. She was becoming more and more convinced that love was one gamble that was worth the risk.

Seventeen

❧❧

Faith felt even shyer than usual as she entered the saloon, as she soon discovered she and Lord Frederick were the cynosure of all eyes. He realized it, too, and holding Faith by his side when she would have scurried away, cleared his throat and said, "Your attention, please. Faith and I would like to announce our betrothal."

There was a volley of good wishes and Faith was released from Frederick's side so that she could run over and receive a hug from Lady Burke, who offered to help Faith with the wedding arrangements. When Lady Burke made her offer Faith felt as if she could explode from happiness; not only was she engaged to the most marvelous man in the world, but Lady Burke was not to disappear from her life just because Faith was not marrying her son.

Sir Anthony very sincerely offered Frederick his congratulations, relieved he was not to be the groom. Then he said, a little too loudly, "It's too bad the game was pronounced forfeit, as I'd have liked to have seen you sweat a little. I doubt you'd be so happily engaged right now if it hadn't been called off."

Diana Perrywhistle, sitting by her beloved's side, heard Sir Anthony's comment. "I knew there was a game!" she exclaimed, before covering her mouth, wishing she could withdraw her words. Faith had looked up at her pronouncement, and Diana was reminded of the awful trick she'd played on her. "That is, I'm sure it was all in fun," she hurried to add, hoping to make amends for her previous behavior.

Frederick knew an explanation was required, as now every female member of the house party was beside themselves with curiosity, and Faith was not looking quite so happy as she had a moment ago.

"The game was quite innocent; the rules being that before a proposal could be made the applicant for the lady's hand had to pass a test, wherein he answered questions about his intended bride. The Captain graciously waived this requirement when I asked for Faith's hand, but I find I would like to be tested, for I wager that I can answer every question posed to me about Faith correctly," Frederick said, smiling at his betrothed. Faith smiled back, relieved to finally have a full explanation about the infamous game and finding it not heinous in the least, but actually somewhat flattering. Then she wondered if Frederick did, in fact, know her so well. She did not think she could make a similar boast about him.

"Done! What's the wager?" Sir Anthony asked.

"It was a figure of speech, Anthony. I hadn't really intended to wager."

Sir Anthony felt this very unfair of his friend, but then Cherry whispered to Anthony that she'd bet him on the outcome, if he'd give her odds of three to one.

"Who would like to be the first to question me?" Frederick asked, and Lydia immediately rose to the occasion, asking, "What is her favorite color?"

"Green," Frederick answered, and everyone

looked at Faith, who nodded.

"Her favorite pastime?" Lady Burke asked.

"Reading, followed by music," Lord Frederick answered.

The interrogation continued, and Frederick astounded the company by reciting Faith's favorite composer, author, poet, and Bible verses.

Diana, who was watching the proceedings with a great deal of amusement while covertly holding Mr. Foster's hand behind a sofa cushion, turned to him and whispered, "Do you know my favorite author, poet, or verses?"

"Do you mean to tell me you *read*, my dear?" Mr. Foster asked, and Diana laughed.

"Not too often," she said, "but I have fond hopes that once we are married I will read a great deal more."

"And I had hoped I would be reading a great deal less," Mr. Foster replied. There was a glint in his eyes Diana was beginning to recognize, and she was amazed to find she was blushing. She, Diana Perrywhistle! How her London friends would tease her if they knew. But they would have to come to Kenilworth if they wanted to see her, because Diana was never letting Edmund Foster out of her sight. She would move in with her cousin, if necessary, until she got him to the altar.

"I am never letting you out of my clutches," Diana told him, not even attempting to hide her designing nature, since it was of no use, anyway.

"My dear Diana, I would not try to escape you. I am determined to follow the counsel of St. Paul, in his first epistle to the Corinthians, chapter 7 verse 9."

"You know I'm no Bible scholar. What does that say?"

"'It is better to marry than to burn,'" he quoted, bringing her hand out from behind the cushion and up to his lips. She had no idea the Bible could be so on point, as her hand felt positively *singed* where he'd kissed it. She looked around to see if anyone had noticed, but they were all still shouting questions at Lord Frederick, and even James had entered the game.

"What was the name of her governess?" James asked.

Lord Frederick was finally silenced. Cherry, who was sure she was about to win her bet, was annoyed with James Perrywhistle. "What does it matter what the name of her governess was?"

"Well, I know the answer," James replied. "It was Miss Biddleton, from Middleton," he announced, and everyone turned to look inquiringly at Faith except for Cherry, who knew he'd answered correctly. When Faith nodded there was a smattering of applause, and James looked quite pleased with himself. Miss Foster even turned to ask him, "Mr. Perrywhistle, how did you ever know such a thing?"

The game ended at that point as the Captain, annoyed that all this nonsense had interrupted his card game just as he was about to win, stated that he, too, had an announcement.

Faith and Cherry exchanged wondering glances, Faith speculating that perhaps her father had managed to win Lady Burke's hand after all.

"Sir Anthony, you have a promising young chap

working in your stables, his name is Tom. Excellent figure, good breadth of arm and wonderful elasticity in the wrists. I have been training him and he could be the next Tom Cribb, except better, as your Tom is not so slow as Cribb is. What d'you say? Will you permit me to take him back with me to Eaton Park for further training?"

Sir Anthony looked over at Cherry. "Certainly, Captain, on the condition that I am able to visit him regularly at your estate and keep an eye on his progress."

"Of course; you're welcome any time. Any time at all."

Cherry smiled at Sir Anthony and he winked at her, before whispering in her ear, "You'd better feed me something other than undercooked beef and stale bread, my girl, or I'll never come to visit you."

"Your constitution's been ruined by all these rich foods," she taunted, before taking a bite of apple tart.

"So, Faith," Lord Frederick said, grabbing her by the hand and dragging her to a private corner of the room, behind a screen. "I've come to collect my winnings."

"Being unaware of the terms of the game, I can be under no obligation to award you anything, sir," Faith told him. "You forget; I am the daughter of a gamester, and so cannot be easily bamboozled by gull-catchers like yourself."

"The original award was to be your hand but since I've won that already, I was thinking you might reward me with another of your, ahem, members. Perhaps a kiss for each correct answer? Surely I deserve some prize for my comprehensive knowledge of your habits, hobbies, and concerns."

"And should James Perrywhistle receive a similar reward?" Faith asked, staring innocently at him.

"How could you so quickly forget your promise, Faith?" Lord Frederick asked, hypnotized by that grey-eyed stare. "You're to kiss no one but me."

"Only you," Faith agreed, and forgetting her shyness, stood on tip-toe to bestow on him his reward.

Epilogue
୨◦ଓ

Faith was delighted to find herself at Kenilworth again almost exactly one year later, and looked lovingly over at her husband of nine months as the carriage entered the grounds.

"Isn't it exciting, Frederick?" she asked him, a smile trembling on her lips.

"What, my lady, is so exciting? Your sister's wedding? The opportunity to hear Mr. Foster's sermons once again? Or perhaps the prospect of a walk in the famous gardens?" he asked, bringing her hand to his lips.

"All the activities you mentioned sound very appealing," Faith replied, "but if you were to accompany me on my walk then I would prefer that activity above all else."

"A walk with you in the gardens is an attractive prospect, I agree, but there is another activity I prefer more," Frederick said, a wicked twinkle in his eyes.

Faith was no longer shy with Frederick, not after nine months of marriage, but she found to her dismay she still blushed very easily. However, since Frederick claimed he loved to see her blush, she couldn't regret the tendency too much.

The doctor had confirmed just recently that she was in an interesting condition, and while happy at the prospect of welcoming their child into the world, she had hoped for a few more months uninterrupted bliss with her new husband. In fact, after the initial excitement of learning they were to have a child had worn off, Faith had retired to bed that evening and indulged in a fit of tears, sad to think that the intimacy she'd so enjoyed was at an end, at least until the time came when they wanted a second child.

Frederick had entered her room to find her crying into a pillow and he had taken her into his arms, asking her what was wrong.

"'Tis silly of me, I suppose, but I had hoped we'd have more time together," Faith told him, after he'd tenderly wiped away her tears.

"Are you planning on leaving me?" Frederick asked jokingly, his expression a little concerned, none-the-less.

"No, of course not. Never!" Faith told him, and she was happy to see his look of concern fade.

"And since I have no intention of ever leaving your side, I can't imagine what you mean."

"I mean, now that I'm *enceinte*, we will no longer..." Faith found it difficult to express her meaning. "You know."

"No, I don't know. Had you supposed I would no longer come to your bed?"

"Well, yes. Now that we've achieved our purpose, surely there's no need?"

"You're mistaken, Faith. There's every need," he'd told her, his brown eyes looking very dark in the candlelight before he drew her into his arms. Faith was thrilled to find that she'd been completely wrong regarding her husband's intentions. It appeared, in her husband's view at least, the child was just a welcome consequence of a pursuit he wholeheartedly enjoyed, and had no intention of curtailing.

But she was truly wicked to be considering such matters now, as their carriage drew up in front of the house. Frederick, whose thoughts appeared to be running parallel to hers, planted a too-quick kiss on her lips before straightening her bonnet and preceding her from the carriage, making it clear he intended to assist her down himself. His hands carefully spanned her waist as he lifted her gently to the ground, and Faith was happy that she was still so early in her pregnancy that her waist was almost as small as the day they'd met. Kenilworth could not but bring back memories of their courtship, and she wanted to relive that time before taking on the duties, and joys, of motherhood.

When she recalled with what trepidation she'd approached this house on her first visit she wanted to laugh out loud, though she realized if she wasn't fortunate enough to have married Frederick she would have little cause for mirth. While her expectations for a husband were admittedly not high, he'd completely exceeded them. He had not lied to Faith when he told her he viewed a wife as a confidant and friend. He frequently sought her opinion on estate matters and other issues, and he spent a great deal of time with her, so much so that she knew he'd spoken truthfully when he told her he desired her company above all others.

While he still enjoyed the hunt and occasionally attended a boxing match or horse race with Captain Wentworth or Sir Anthony, she was relieved that he was not a gamester like her father. Shortly after their marriage her father had been forced to let Eaton Park, as his gambling losses had exceeded his income. The Captain had moved into a small cottage on the grounds of his estate, but spent most of his time visiting his married daughter at her new home or, after his younger daughter's betrothal to Sir Anthony, joining Cherry on visits to Kenilworth.

Faith would have been surprised to learn that her father had missed his daughters more than he'd anticipated, and it was for this reason more than any other he was such a frequent visitor.

After she and Lord Frederick had entered the house and were announced to Lady Burke, Faith was delighted to see not only that dear lady awaiting their arrival, but also Sir Anthony, Cherry, Captain Wentworth, Mr. Foster and his wife, Diana. The only ones missing from the original party were the Perrywhistles and Miss Foster, who were expected to arrive later that day.

"Isn't it exciting, Faith?" Cherry said, grabbing her sister and kissing her enthusiastically on the cheek while unknowingly echoing her sister's words. "I'm to be married in two days! Who would have ever dreamt we'd one day be *married*?"

"Apparently Lord Frederick and Sir Anthony had hopes of such an outcome," Diana said.

Faith was surprised to see Diana looking so domesticated. Her smile seemed totally sincere, and she'd even gained a little weight. Faith wondered if Diana could also be in an interesting condition.

"And don't forget Mrs. Tibbet," Cherry said. "She was determined to see us all wed, also, but not to each other."

"Tibbet," said Sir Anthony, with a shudder. "Please don't mention the name. I'd hoped never to be reminded of her again."

"I am so sorry to hear that, dearest Anthony, as I invited her to the wedding."

"What? Why?"

"Well, even though it was an unintended result of her machinations, it's true that without her efforts the four of us would not have met," Cherry explained, and Sir Anthony had to admit the truth of that statement. "Besides, she gave me an invaluable piece of advice that I'm convinced helped me win you."

"What advice?" Sir Anthony asked.

"She told me the brawnier the gentleman, the softer his brain," Cherry said, with a smile to show she was merely teasing.

"What nonsense!" Sir Anthony cried, while the Captain also voiced his displeasure. Diana and Mr. Foster merely grinned at each other, while Lord Frederick, not quite as brawny as Sir Anthony or the Captain, sized each man up, wondering if Tibbet's theory might actually have some validity.

"I think her other bit of advice to you was even better," Faith said.

"Really? What was that?" Cherry asked.

"To sit up straight, as no gentleman wants to marry a hunchback," Faith said. "I've embroidered it onto a seat cover."

"It was a good thing I engaged that woman; she was well worth the expense," the Captain said, unaware that Faith was joking, and thinking how satisfactorily everything had worked out. Both his daughters were more than creditably settled, thanks to him. Now if only he could convince his newest son-in-law to honeymoon in Ireland, his joy would be complete. The Captain had been tipped off about a promising filly, and was sure Sir Anthony would be thrilled to purchase her, for a price that included the Captain's finder's fee.

Captain Wentworth racked his brain to think of a way he could persuade Sir Anthony, when he suddenly realized Cherry would be delighted to learn of the filly's bloodlines and would be far more effective in convincing Sir Anthony than he would. How fortunate for him that he had a daughter who took an interest in such things.

Watching Faith and Charity sitting side by side, discussing the upcoming wedding, it occurred to the Captain that a man couldn't ask for two more wonderful daughters. When he felt his eyes becoming a little moist, he excused himself from the drawing room and went to spar with his groom in the stables, before setting out on a twenty mile walk.

He might be nearing fifty, but he was still the Celebrated Pedestrian.

The End

Author's Note

The character Captain Richard Standham Wentworth in this novel was inspired by the real-life Celebrated Pedestrian, Robert Barclay, one of the most famous men of his time. He wagered he could walk 1000 miles in 1000 hours for 1000 pounds, and successfully completed this feat on July 12, 1809. Fortunes were made and lost on that day, as The Times reported that the total of all bets placed on the event was 100,000 pounds, estimated to be about 40 million pounds in today's money.

For more information about Barclay and other members of The Fancy, the group of gentlemen sportsmen in the Regency era, please read Peter Radford's book *The Celebrated Captain Barclay: Sport, Gambling and Adventure in Regency Times.*

Made in the USA
Monee, IL
01 August 2020

37408287R00121